In Good Company

volume seven

In Good Company

volume seven

A Short Story Collection

Edited
by
Patricia Adler

Editorial Assistant: Alexandria Tirrigan

Copyright © 2009
by Live Wire Press

"The Red Dress" copyright ©2009, Matt Cutugno

Edited by Patricia Adler

All rights reserved for one year from copyright date,
including the right to reproduce this work
in any form whatsoever, without permission
in writing from the publisher, except for brief passages
in connection with a review.

Cover art © Istockphoto.com

For information call:
Live Wire Press
103 Birdwood Court
Charlottesville, VA 22903
e-mail: arieseagle@gmail.com
Web site: www.livewirepress.net
or www.livewirepress.wordpress.com

If you are unable to order this book from your local bookseller,
you may order directly from the publisher.

Library of Congress Control Number: 99-067352
ISBN 978-0-9727531-8-0

10 9 8 7 6 5 4 3 2 1

Printed in the United States

To the awesome potential of all creation.

Publisher's Note

It is with great pleasure that Live Wire Press brings you volume seven of this series. The raison d'être of *In Good Company* is to surround a featured author with lesser-known or unpublished writers, thus putting them "in good company."

We begin with *The Red Dress*, an unpublished short story by our featured author, Matt Cutugno.

Enjoy . . .

Patricia S. Adler
Publisher

Table of Contents

The Red Dress 1
    Matt Cutugno

Conrad's Passage 17
    Don Amburgey

Second Act 23
    Jason Atkins

The Gardener 30
    Terry Cox-Joseph

The Day a Crow Snatched My Baby Sister 38
    Pete Freas

The Door of Randolph Manor 43
    Stephanie Friar

Sitting on Plastic 56
    Doris Gwaltney

The Pony That Looked West 62
    Elaine Habermehl

Watch Birds 64
    Elaine Habermehl

Rainy Night in Wilhering 70
    Keppel Hagerman

The Husky Young Man and the Nun 75
    Robert Kelly

The Caregiver 82
    M.L. Kline

The Monkey Man 87
    D. S. Lliteras

The Left Ascension 95
    D. S. Lliteras

Summer 1956 98
    Jim Meehan

From a Distance, through the Foliage 103
    Anne Meek

No Danger to Self or Others 115
    Anne Meek

Josie Higgins 123
    Lu Motley

When Fate Comes Calling 129
    Sandra Ratcliff

Needin' Mista Sun 145
    Lynn Veach Sadler

The Most Beautiful Music 156
    Shirley Nesbitt Sellers

About the Authors 163

The Red Dress

Matt Cutugno

It was not a match made in heaven; heaven would not have it. They met one night at Karaoke when he got up and sang a Jay Chou song, and with his naturally high voice, he really sounded like the Taiwanese heartthrob. She was in the back of the room, pressed up against the wall. She was waiting for someone like him; she sized him up and decided right then and there. Making her way to near where he was sitting, she positioned herself such that when he looked away from the stage, he would see her. When he did, she smiled.

"Hello there," he said.

"Yes," she intoned, as if that was a proper reply.

"My name is Wei," he said in Mandarin.

"Yes," she said again and offered her hand, which he took and held. She had a face that might best be described as interesting. She had straight black hair, dark eyes, and full lips, but her eyes didn't quite match each other, one being placed ever so slightly lower on her face than the other, and that eye's eyelid being ever so slightly more closed. It gave her a permanent quizzical look, as if she wasn't quite sure of what she was seeing in the world around her. Her body language was striking: sitting on the bar stool as if it were a throne, she held one arm flat on the bar, ready to wave at subordinates.

"What's your name," he asked. She blushed momentarily.

"I really can't say," she said in Mandarin with an accent he knew was from the south.

He did not respond. He just looked at her, and she allowed him. He thought she was pretty—taller than many Asian girls, and slim. The cooler she acted, the more attractive he found her.

"I can't tell you my name . . . yet," she leaned in and said to him.

"Why can't you?"

"Because I am famous in China," she said with a sigh of relief, as if she had gotten something off her chest. He was born and raised in China, and had no reason to believe she was famous, but the girl had struck his fancy, and fame is relative.

"Ah, that's nice," he replied.

So it began. They left Karaoke together that night, and walked the four blocks to his apartment in Flushing, Queens. He was happy when she came up to see his place, surprised that she sat on the couch so close to him, and awed when she reached out, held his shirt, and brought him to her mouth. This was new; he was a young man who was neither adept at nor lucky in the ways of romance.

"We are a fine match," she said in the morning, and her words seemed wise beyond any further reflection. She told him her name was Ja, and pointed out what he already knew—that Ja can mean "the one" in Chinese.

"My name means different things," he said. She held a finger up in a gesture of clarification.

"It means 'great'—that's a lot of pressure for you to live up to," she said and then enjoyed a laugh. He didn't seem to mind being an object of ridicule. She was like some drug. Wei had never taken drugs in his life. This feeling was making him understand addiction.

They were together constantly for five days and nights after the evening they met at Karaoke. They flew to Las Vegas that weekend and got married. A few friends, and his uncle who lived in Manhattan, expressed concern when Wei shared the news. He responded to them all the same way, saying that Ja was sent to him by a kind spirit at the behest of an all-knowing God. He even quoted her.

"She and I are a fine match," he'd say, as if he were a diamond-cutter examining two earrings instead of a newlywed husband.

Even such a man might have suspected Ja was less than angelic the night after their wedding ceremony when they were having dinner at the Venetian Casino in Las Vegas. Not long after they had begun eating, she slammed down the spoon she was using, and waved frantically for the waiter.

"This bird's nest soup tastes like pee water," she said in English with her heavy accent. The waiter, thin and craggily faced, did not understand.

"Pee water?"

Her face got red. "Pee water, you stupid, what you make when you pee."

Wei was embarrassed by the attention she attracted. He led her away, leaving cash on the table before the meal was finished. Ja stormed out, clutching at her shawl like some threatened queen at the advance of liegemen.

When they were alone in bed that night, she cried. Softly at first, then with growing sobs, then in residing sniffles. She told her husband that in China her parents abused her. Her father was a drinker who would strike her, and her mother would take money that Ja made working after school.

"How cruel is this world," she intoned, "if someone as innocent as I can be hurt so many times?"

He was touched by her words and he wanted to be as kind as he had ever been. "That's terrible," he said.

"You must help me all my life," she whispered and pulled him on top of herself. Wei's mind was lost in the night's swirl of sights and sounds of the Strip. It was as if he were standing in line at the most exciting of amusement park rides, with his two hands full of tickets.

Wei worked as a banker in Manhattan and had a solid, stable job, so money was not a problem. She moved into his apartment in Flushing. She soon proved she was no homemaker. While she had ready opinions on how her new husband should sit at the dinner table, she did not seem to care if old pillowcases, held over windows with push pins, served as drapes, or if dirty dishes piled high in the kitchen sink. She hired a maid, and her husband paid for the service.

She opened a bank account for herself in her hometown in China, and had her husband give her $20,000 to put in it. "This will be my dowry," she said, holding up the passbook. Wei understood that a dowry was something a bride brought to her husband's estate, so he was confused but was silent.

One evening, he found her writing in a small black book as she lay in bed with a box of chocolates. He had noticed her writing in the same book before.

"What are you doing?" he asked, in a sweet a tone of voice.

"Oh, nothing, secrets," she said.

He was playful. "I thought husbands and wives should have no secrets."

"Who told you that?"

"I don't know."

"Well then."

"People say that."

"You must have that mixed up with something else people say."

"Maybe I do."

"Women must have secrets, it is essential that they do."

"Why?"

"For our own protection."

"Yes," was all he said.

She felt the need to explain: "Because the world is against us and we must fight back." She poked the little book at him for emphasis as she spoke. He thought there was no logic in her words, but she had great conviction, and that impressed him. Wei left her to her writing.

Days later, when he came home from work, he found his wife at the sofa in the living room. On the sofa was a pile of clothes and other items.

"What are these?" she said to him the very moment he walked in the door. He put down his briefcase, and looked at the things on the sofa. They belonged to a friend of his, Nancy. The two had grown up together in China.

"Those are Nancy's; I told you all about her."

"Your friend, but you did not tell me she had this stuff; I found it all."

"It's just a few things, some clothes, a pair of running shoes she left here—we used to run together."

"These?" she said and she picked up the running shoes and brought them to the sliding glass doors that led outside to a small terrace. She opened the door, took at step outside, and threw the shoes into the night. Their apartment was on the 34th floor overlooking a large parking lot below, so Wei's reaction was predictable.

"Don't do that, we're so high up, someone might get hit with those shoes."

"I don't care."

"Ja, be reasonable, it's nothing."

"Don't say anything I do is nothing."

"What you are doing is dangerous."

"If people are in the parking lot, they should look up when they see shoes coming." With that she took another item from the sofa: a Walkman CD player, headphones still plugged in. She marched back to the open sliding door, and tossed the player over the railing. A dark eternity of time seemed to pass as Wei stood wide eyed until the sound of the Walkman's crash could be heard from below. It likely had hit a car top, because in a moment a car alarm blared out. This made neighborhood dogs bark, which made lights go on in various places. Wei rushed to the sliding doors, closed and locked them. He pulled the long curtains closed. Outside, the car alarm sounded in a shrill cadence.

That night in bed, she cried in his arms. She said she was sorry she threw things off the terrace. She blamed her parents who both have terrible tempers. She told Wei that he was the most important thing in her life and that she was dedicating her life to making him a great man. The two bodies held each other tight, and the wife began to kiss the husband.

"I love you so much," she said.

The next day they went shopping together. It was her idea that they would buy each other something: she would buy him a suit and he would buy her a new dress. He was charmed by the idea; it seemed a sweet thing for newlyweds or any couple to do. So they drove into Manhattan. They went first downtown on the west side, where she picked out for him a navy blue suit with light gray pinstripping. "Perfect for the business meeting," she announced. He dutifully tried it on, and turned around in place at her command. At one point a salesman came by, smiled, and asked if he could be of assistance. Ja waved him away.

"We are very fine thanks so much," she said in accented English not easy to understand. Wei stood in front of a full length mirror and Ja stood behind him looking over his shoulder at the mirrored image.

"You look like a great banker in this," she said to her husband.

Neither Wei (being a young man unaware of how to properly dress himself) nor his wife (who was anxious to move on to her own shopping) noticed that the pants for the pinstriped suit did not quite match the jacket. Apparently a previous shopper, in trying on the jacket, put it back on a hanger with another pair of pants from a similar suit. Even as Wei modeled for his wife the salesman approached them, having noticed that the pin stripping on the pants was slightly thicker than that of the jacket.

"May I point something out?" he asked politely.

"It is never polite to point," Ja said.

So she paid for her husband's suit in cash, and the two left the store. They then drove uptown to a small boutique on Madison Avenue. She picked out an expensive designer dress. It was bright red, her favorite color. It had large black pearl buttons and came with a silver and onyx belt. As he watched her model it for him, the thought occurred to him that perhaps it was a size too small. It clung around her hips and hiked up as she moved so that her hem line was near thigh high. In his private thoughts he imagined that in this dress she was like an expensive prostitute for a powerful man.

"How do I look?" He knew he could not share his thoughts. Instead, he smiled and said in Mandarin "you look like the one," and she understood the pun he was making with her name and she was pleased.

"Husband, I didn't know you were great, and clever," she giggled and then laughed her loud laugh which, to Wei's embarrassment, caught the attention of all in the boutique. But they went home that evening and made passionate love. She whispered in his ear that he was a great lover.

The next day, she asked him for more money to put into her bank account, and, reluctantly, he agreed.

"How much do you want?" he asked. She barely looked up from the bowl of congee she was eating. She poked at it with a spoon, pushing it from one side to the other.

"Twenty thousand dollars please," she said.

"I see," was all he could reply.

"And it's not what I want," she corrected, "It's what we need."

"The bank account is in China."

"I don't want to pay any tax here; I don't think it's fair."

"The account is in your name."

"I have made you the beneficiary."

"Did you?" He was touched.

"I plan on doing that," she offered. He wired money to China that afternoon.

She began arranging vacation getaways for them—short trips upstate for a weekend to Lake George, or a quick flight to the outer banks in North Carolina, then longer trips to Florida and the West Coast. She loved to travel on the arm of her husband, to send him off to the beach so she could shop, then to dine in the evening at a restaurant where she could berate the help when their efforts did not meet her standards.

One evening in Flushing, Wei came home late. He had a business meeting over dinner, then he met Nancy for coffee and dessert at one of the Chinese bakeries on Main Street. He got home just after midnight. Ja was up and in the living room. As Wei walked in, she was pacing. He couldn't help but notice that she was holding a kitchen knife in her hand. She held it blade down, at a menacing angle.

"What's wrong?" he said to her.

"Wrong, what is wrong?" she said in a laughing voice that was anything but funny. "My husband is home late."

"I told you where I was going to be; Nancy had asked if I could help her with . . ."

"Enough," she announced, and even she might have suspected she was sounding like a bad Hong Kong movie because she said not another word. Instead, she lunged at Wei with the knife. He let out a sound, raised up his hands, and stepped back and aside. She moved closer and lunged again, and her swing barely brushed his open sweater. Now he jumped back and ran to the other side of the room.

"What is wrong with you; are you crazy?" he said in his loudest voice, which was hardly a bellow. While he stared intently at her, she stood still, drew in a deep breath, then let out a long sigh. She casually tossed the blade on the sofa, and looked around the room, world weary.

"I'm tired," she said dramatically.

That night, in bed with Wei, she cried again. She said she had been attacked by a classmate with a knife in school back in China. But even as she told the story, his mind was elsewhere. Still shaken by her attack, he was not sympathetic to her tears. She began to touch him, told him how strong a man he was and how much she needed him to be strong, but he did not respond to her touch.

"Good night," she said and rolled away toward the wall. Within moments, she was snoring. Wei, though, did not sleep well that night, with strange dreams dominating his sleep.

Distressing also for him was his wife's business, which she had opened shortly after coming to this country. She had a store front in Flushing that advertised help for new immigrants. She offered services to those who were here illegally and who sought legal status. An honorable enterprise, Wei thought, but then one night he received a phone call at home from a Chinese woman who said Ja took her money and did not perform the promised services. Another time, when he went to pick up his wife at work on a Saturday afternoon, she was arguing with a man.

"Yes you did, you did," Wei heard the man yelling in Mandarin with a Fujianese accent. "You owe me money," he insisted. Ja was cool as could be, sitting at a desk, holding papers in both of her hands, as the man raged around her.

"This is not a proper business, you should not do this," the man said.

She waved at him dismissively. "You are lucky I do not call the police. Now leave, my husband has arrived; he has a temper and he may hurt you," and then she called the man a name in the Fujianese dialect, one Wei recognized as a very bad and low thing to say to someone.

At home, she explained to him that yes, there have been some dissatisfied customers, a very few, but they were all illegal aliens and finally, what could they do? Go to the police? And she laughed her joyless laugh, and her husband nodded, but he did not laugh.

It was after that he spoke with his uncle. The two sat in a restaurant in midtown and it took a long time before the young man could say what was on this mind.

"I may have made a mistake in getting married," he began.

The uncle, a smart and successful businessman, said nothing. He simply listened as his nephew outlined his new wife's mercurial personality. Wei then told of her business ways, which could well be illegal and which were certainly of questionable ethics.

"Has she ever gotten violent with you?" the uncle asked.

"Oh no," Wei said, and his face reddened to betray his lie.

When he got home one night that week, Ja was on the phone. She was speaking Mandarin, and Wei quickly gathered she was speaking to her parents in China. Even while holding the phone with one hand, she waved her other arm about, and was becoming more and more agitated. When she hung up he pretended that he hadn't heard the conversation. She would have none of it.

"I know what you're thinking," she said, even though she could not have known.

Wei felt resignation more than anything else, so he said "I know."

"You do not know."

"Okay, I don't."

"Why are you acting like this? This is unbecoming."

"Unbecoming of what?"

"A husband of mine, I will not allow it," she said. She turned and walked into the kitchenette. When she returned she had a stack of dinner plates and she placed them on an end table. She then picked one up, reached back with it in a way to suggest she had done this before, and threw it at him. He ducked, it flew high, and smashed into pieces against the wall. It took Wei moments to understand.

"That plate, that's my grandmother's plate."

"Is it?" She was unimpressed and grabbed another one from the end table.

"Ja that plate was one hundred years old."

"Not any more it isn't."

"What are you doing?"

She considered him, then looked at the stack of plates. "I was wrong to throw that old plate. Here, this plate was a wedding gift from your uncle, cheap stuff." With that she threw a second plate. This time it hit him in the arm, smashing the plate into pieces. There was a sharp sound, and he gave a cry and grabbed his arm at the elbow.

Ja spent a night in jail for that. Neighbors, hearing arguing and sounds of smashing dinnerware, called the police. By the time officers arrived, the angry wife had thrown and broken a dozen plates. In front of the police, she ranted in both Chinese and English, accusing her husband of everything from cheating on her to stealing her money. The officers saw Wei standing there quietly, holding his left arm up with his right arm. When the police told Ja she was being arrested for domestic assault, she grabbed one last plate, and threw it in the direction of a cop. This last act ended all discussion and civility. She was handcuffed, read her rights, and hauled away. Wei declined the invitation to pay his wife's bail. She claimed to have no money of her own, so she was the overnight guest of the 34th police precinct in Flushing.

Alone in his apartment, Wei had time to reflect. He sat in an easy chair in his living room, and thoughts ran through his mind in crazy randomness. It occurred to him that his wife wanted them to meet that night at Karaoke, that she used him. He decided that yes, he should have gotten to know her better before marriage. The more these thoughts stayed with him, the angrier he got at himself. But while it was true he was an unusually naïve young man, he was also smart. He could not be made a complete fool. That afternoon he consulted with a lawyer in Manhattan.

When Ja was released from the precinct holding cell the next afternoon, a man greeted her on the street with: "Hello there, may I have a word?" He was holding an envelope.

"What do you want?" she said to him as she looked him up and down. He was young, Latin, tall and thin. He wore business attire.

"This is for you," he said and offered the envelope. Slowly, a look came over her face as she stared at the boy and the envelope. The look started as indifference then became realization. She put both her hands up in the air, said "No, I don't want it," and hurried off in the opposite direction. The server of the divorce papers followed for a step or two then stopped. He knew what likely Ja did not—that such legal papers have to merely be presented. The recipient does not have to take them. By running off, she accomplished nothing. Her divorce papers were served.

She moved out of their apartment and stayed with a friend who lived across the park in Corona. The couple agreed to attempt reconciliation, meeting at a restaurant on Roosevelt Avenue. Things started amicably enough.

"Husband, you look well," she said.

"You too," Wei said, though plain was the feeling that neither meant it. She began by asking him if all this divorce talk was necessary and if they could possibly work out any differences. He might have been agreeable to that, but Ja's attitude betrayed any sincerity on her part. She intently ate as they spoke.

"You don't seem very interested in being a good wife," Wei said in a way to suggest he was perceptive, though he was not. Ja acted stunned, and she was an actor.

"Have you been a good husband?" she asked and batted her eyes.

Wei was prepared; he took a breath and spoke as if reciting. "I have loved you, married you, and provided a place to live. I pay all your bills, some of which are mine too because we are man and wife. On two occasions, I gave you $20,000. In return, you hate my friends, you won't even have dinner with my uncle because you think he didn't give us enough money for our wedding."

"Are you finished?"

"I am not finished; I can go on."

"Do not bother."

"I thought we were going to talk?"

"Wei, you child."

"Don't call me that."

"You understand what you get being married to me?"

"What?"

"Don't what me. You get so much it's not even funny."

"What are you talking about?" he asked and she just smiled and ran a hand through her hair then tossed her head back.

"Are you talking about sex?" he said, surprised the words came out of his mouth.

"I give you my body to play with. You knew nothing before you met me. Now you're better."

He was not a young man who could bear such discourse. He did not know what to say in response, so he could not answer. Instead, he left the restaurant (after leaving cash on the table for the meal).

Divorce proceedings began. Wei wanted to be as civil as possible. He found out that New York does not have No Fault Divorce, so his papers were filed on the grounds of "Extreme Cruelty." He was the Petitioner, and Ja was the Respondent. There were initial meetings with lawyers, then follow-ups. There would be depositions, and affidavits, and Affirmations in Opposition. Ja found a lawyer in Queens. His name was Donny Choo. He was a slightly built, middle-aged man from Hong Kong, who was thin on top and a bit slope shouldered. But he was smart and prided himself in being as ruthless as legally possible.

"If a client of mine does not want to win huge, then Mr. Choo is not the lawyer for them," he said to Ja at their first meeting. His tough talk was music to her ears.

The two of them prepared a case in which indeed there was "Fault," and it was Wei's. Mr. Choo filed for Abandonment. Wei had abandoned Ja in every sense: literally, as they lived apart; physically, as they had not had sexual relations since the plate incident; more importantly, financially; and most importantly, emotionally. It was in illustrating this last thing that Ja invested herself. She was a young woman who was born to play the victim. She could soften, lower her gaze, she could hold her hands sedately in her lap as she sat.

Wei, for his part, tried to prepare for his ultimate day in court. His lawyer was a woman; her name was Annette. She was smart enough, and experienced. If she seemed to Wei to perhaps lack a certain passion, he felt confident that she would do a good job. After all, he had evidence of his wife's cruelty, of her extreme personality.

Mr. Choo filed an Affirmation in Opposition, and in it Ja claimed she had zero income. That's $0.00. She stated that Wei occasionally beat her, and forced her to have sexual relations, and that he used the fact that he spoke English much better than she did to convince the police in Flushing that she was to blame for the domestic ruckus that got her arrested. The issue of anti-Asian prejudice was raised, underlined by the fact that Wei was an American citizen and Ja was not. In his submitted papers, Mr. Choo asked the Court to grant the aggrieved wife $2,500 a month in alimony payments, plus a one time payment of $100,000. Wei was sickened as he read.

Wei and his lawyer had some difficulties finding a legal trail to the monies that Wei gave to his wife during their marriage. The Chinese banking system is less accountable than ours, and it was proving difficult to refute Ja's claim that the money went to pay medical bills for her poor family in China. Further, it was proving difficult to show that Ja ran a business in Flushing, or to find former or current customers who were dissatisfied with her efforts or were cheated by her. Wei visited the storefront that had served as his wife's business and it wasn't there—she had moved with no trace.

One evening, Wei received a phone call on his cell from an unknown number. It was Ja.

"How is your case going?" she asked.

"You know I can't talk about it."

"I see, too bad. Do you want to know how my case is going?"

"No."

"My case is going fantastic, Donny Choo is a genius." She had a tone in her voice; it was self-satisfaction, and Wei found it both angering and depressing. Shouldn't divorce be a traumatic experience? Oughtn't it to result in sleepless nights of soul searching?

Shortly after that, his lawyer, Annette, went on maternity leave. She would not be able to make the scheduled day in court. She had done a competent job, and the pieces of Wei's case were in place. She was replaced by another lawyer, a man, and Wei did not have such a good impression of him. First of all, he was bald and rotund, which did not seem ideal physical appearance for a lawyer. Annette was an attractive woman, someone who could stand in front of a judge and stylishly say "Your Honor, don't let my client's so-called wife get away with this!"

Further, Wei's new attorney—his name was Leo—had a habit of grunting. After he finished a sentence or when he leaned across a table for court papers, he would let out a hard breath and make a sharp sound. It was not a very noticeable thing, but it was odd enough that Wei was sure the judge would notice, be annoyed at Wei because of it, and hold it against him. All these negative elements became like a slow-moving wave crashing down over him. A feeling of dread arrived, and he could not shake it.

Wei was not, in general, a thoughtful boy, but he was becoming one. This wave that was upon him made him think about life—his in particular. He was not religious, but thought of himself as spiritual, and he wondered what spirit had he offended to be in this position. Hadn't his wife been sent by God to enrich their common lives? If not, then what spirit did send her?

One rainy day in spring, with angry gray clouds above him, Wei entered the District Court building in downtown Manhattan. He walked into room 8A on the second floor. The room was small, and empty, and he sat in the first row and looked at the judge's raised bench and the long narrow tables where would sit Petitioner and Respondent and their lawyers. He listened to the profound silence. He wore his mismatched navy blue suit, which he had just had dry cleaned. His white shirt was over-starched, and he pulled the collar away from his skin.

A uniformed clerk came in, nodded at Wei, and began setting up for court. The Petitioner sat there a little shocked that this day had finally arrived. He tried to keep the weather out of his mind because bad weather could be a bad omen. And he tried not to think of his lawyer and any shortcomings. Wei's uncle told him that the laws of karma would prevail. But the young man had no such faith in karma. He had only fragile hope.

Another court officer came into the room. He said hello to the first, then stopped to let out a noisy yawn. He adjusted the microphone at the judge's bench. Then the room's front door opened and Leo walked in and waved at his client.

"Wei, ready for your big day?"

That seemed like an odd thing to say. A wedding day is one's "big day." It's exciting, enjoyable. This was as far removed from that as the mind of God is from the evil that men do.

"I am ready," Wei said, and tugged in turn at both sleeves of his jacket.

Just then Donny Choo and Ja came into the room. They seemed to be in an animated, whispering conversation as they did, then stopped as they arrived at the table. Her lawyer greeted Leo.

"My friend, nice to see you," he said and the two shook hands politely. Mr. Choo did not acknowledge Wei and neither did his client. Wei was surprised when he saw her because Ja was wearing her red dress and had a small matching purse. She held her head high as she had a seat.

Wei did not know what to do with himself. He thought it seemed far too quiet for a small room with half a dozen people in it. That was a bad sign. Wei watched Leo arrange some papers, then listened to the giggling of Choo and Ja, and wondered what they could possibly find so funny. Just then, the stenographer came into the room and made her way to her small desk and prepared herself for a day's work in court. She took out from a drawer the shorthand machine she would use to record the proceedings.

After a bit, the judge entered the room. His name was Brooks, and he was tall and thin, wore rather thick glasses, and had a head full of bushy, unkempt hair. He sat at his desk and took a deep, quiet breath, then looked over the four in front of him.

"Counselor," he said to Leo.

"Your Honor," Wei's lawyer replied.

"Counselor," the judge said to Ja's attorney.

"Your Honor," Donny Choo said, drawing out the two words and smiling as if the two were old friends. At that, Judge Brooks opened a Redweld file folder on his desk. He removed papers relevant to the case. He then slowly laid them in some order on the desk.

Wei had a bad feeling. The judge looked up and in the direction of Ja, and out of the corner of his eye Wei could see Ja smiling and running a hand through her hair. The woman had no conscience, and she was winning.

After what seemed like an eternity, Leo raised a hand.

"Your Honor, may I point something out?" he said.

The judge did not look up. Instead, he held a flat hand up to the lawyer and kept reading and arranging. Wei was annoyed at Leo—don't interrupt the man he wanted to shout.

Time was standing still. Wei could hear the wall clock ticking, then he noted the beating of his own heart. He felt a single drop of perspiration running down his cheek, and he touched his face with his hand to stop it. He pondered this moment in his life, and how every moment before contributed to now. The judge interrupted his musings.

"Will the Petitioner and the Respondent come up here and stand before me?"

Wei unbuttoned his jacket, stood up from his seat, and walked around the table to the judge's bench. By the time he arrived, his suit jacket had been buttoned back up. Ja stood up, tugged her dressed down, and stepped forward. The dress, originally a size too small, was now two sizes too small. Too, she had failed to have the garment dry cleaned, so it had a wrinkly appearance. As Wei watched her, he thought that she still looked like a prostitute, but now like one who worked for less, and in bad neighborhoods.

Judge Brooks examined a single page of paper. He looked at Wei.

"Wei?"

"Yes." The judge then looked at Ja.

"Ja?"

She smiled back, said "Yes," and nodded hello.

There in front of the judge stood two people that he could not help but feel some pity for. One was a young man, looking lost, in a suit that found its jacket not matching its pants. And there was a young woman, confident and friendly, in a tight red dress.

Time slowed down again. Judge Brooks looked at Wei, then at the paper in his hand, then at Ja, then at more papers. He adjusted his glasses. Suddenly, Ja spoke and pointed.

"I bought that suit for him, that one he is wearing today." At that Donny Choo gently stood up, but the judge waved him back into his seat. The jurist looked at Wei's suit—from his nicely cut jacket collar down to his pants. He noticed slightly scuffed shoes too.

"Did you really?" he asked of the Respondent.

"Yes," she replied and was proud. The jurist took a long moment and considered her. Then, just as decisively, he returned his full attention to the case.

"In the decision of this court, I find for the Petitioner," he decreed. "The divorce is granted. I further provide for a one time payment of $5,000 to the Respondent, payable immediately. I deem no alimony."

Each of the four concerned who stood before the judge let out a gasp. Wei could not believe the words he just heard, and in fact wasn't sure he heard correctly; Ja clutched her chest and looked at her lawyer, who stood up and whispered something to her. Leo was, with a grunt, also on his feet.

"Your Honor, may I speak?" Donny Choo inquired.

The judge smiled. "Mr. Choo, you may not; it's going to be a very busy morning. We have a marriage here of short duration, with no children or joint property, and I've read the police report. I've made my decision. Have a pleasant day one and all," he said and motioned to the clerk behind him. Judge Brooks stood up, straightened his black robe, and left the room, but not before he took a last look at the Respondent with an ever-so-slight shake of his bushy-haired head.

Wei and Ja and their lawyers remained standing exactly as they stood when the court's judgment was announced. One of the uniformed clerks left, then after a moment, the stenographer did. Ja began to speak to Donny Choo in Mandarin, in whispers at first then in a voice increasingly loud. "What kind of court is this?" she wanted to know. She theorized that Judge Brooks was gay, and that he naturally hates women. She offered that perhaps Wei's homely bald lawyer had bribed the judge. Mr. Choo kindly retorted that none of that could possibly be the case. Ja started to leave, then stopped and turned to her ex-husband. Far too proud a woman to show much feeling, she nonetheless had a look on her face that Wei found refreshing: she was humiliated, and she glowed a fine shade of embarrassment, as red as her dress. She stormed out, first pushing a chair aside. Mr. Choo was at her high heels, telling Ja in Mandarin that they needed to talk about his bill. This too made Wei feel fine.

Alone with Leo, the two shared a nervous laugh at all that had just happened. The last court clerk was finishing a phone call. Then he straightened up some papers, locked a desk drawer, and departed. Room 8A was empty save the two.

"I guess . . . we did all right," Leo said, acknowledging the great understatement. Wei began to laugh, quietly at first, but then in a near guffaw of happy emotion. Leo enjoyed the moment too, and they gave each other a hug and patted each other's back.

"Wei, we got lucky; sometimes that's better than being smart," Leo said. The two shook hands, the victorious lawyer left, and the newly divorced young man was alone but not lonely. He felt strange, strangely exhilarated. He sat down and unbuttoned the jacket of his suit. He slowly rolled his head on his neck and shoulders; he took a deep breath and exhaled.

Then and there, Wei decided he could never think of his life in quite the same way after this day. He felt better than lucky, he felt blessed. He promised himself that he would make better life decisions, that he would be kinder to strangers. When he walked outside onto Centre Street in lower Manhattan, the rain had stopped. A growing band of sunlight was trying to break through the cloud cover, and Wei had no doubt that it would.

Could all of this have come about because of an ill-fitting red dress? If so, that can be called magnificent irony, and is one of the proofs of the existence of God.

Conrad's Passage

Don Amburgey

"Come on, come on, baby, stop me! Stop me!" Conrad heard Rantsom Baker's taunting voice. "Chick, chick, chick, feed him grit."

Dribbling the basketball over the freshly varnished gym floor, Rantsom tried to drive around Conrad to the basket.

"Move it!" Coach Roberts shouted at Rantsom. "Get that smirk off your face, now!"

"Yes, I'll stop you Rant, always on guard against your kind. You learn name calling in the coal camps?" Conrad, a freshman in high school, retorted, gasping for air.

Rantsom danced and stomped at the floor like a hostile gamecock, trying head fakes left and right. Conrad stood his ground.

"You can't score over me, Rantsom," Conrad said.

"Watch me chicken. I'm driving straight to the hoop," Rantsom bragged.

Conrad could see Rantsom's flailing arms and skinny legs in jittery action: stepping backward then forward, bobbing and weaving like a hackling bantam. Conrad dogged his every footstep.

"Beanie," Rantsom shouted. "Or should I say tushhog?"

"Wipe the egg off your mouth, Rant." Conrad could play the game of insults, too.

"Rant, Rant, or should I say RAT!"

Conrad saw Rantsom's hostile gray eyes tracking him. He pivoted left, he pivoted right on the dribble; Rantsom could not be shaken off. The referee's whistle stopped the action.

Resting on the bleachers beside Rantsom, Conrad listened to the next group of scrimmaging freshmen; their shoes squeaked against the floor.

Coach Roberts stalked the sidelines barking orders: "Get those hands up, stick to your man, watch his feet!" The coach stood well over six feet tall with large, ham-fisted hands.

Conrad began to dislike the coach; he was too much like a growling bulldog. Then, he heard Rantsom's raucous voice: "Bring out the lettuce and tomato." Burning memories of shame flashed back from grade school days: his name had so often invited classmates to sing: "Here comes old Mr. Hamburger, Amberger!"

Being the younger of two brothers, Conrad had been called "Baby Hamburger." But, that score could always be settled off court.

"Better to eat lettuce and tomato than coal dust in the mining camps," Conrad shot back. "Yes, it's even better than a baker's dozen spoons of miner's strawberries!"

He saw Rantsom's face screw up.

"Tell you this, Conrad, I'm here to play varsity ball."

"That why your dad moved you from Hardburleigh?"

"Right. But lots of people move around these days."

Conrad wanted a high school diploma above everything else in life. His mother, Francie, before she died, had said he would be the one to go to college like Uncle Gifford. His uncle was the brainy one, winning statewide honors for outstanding educational achievements. For Conrad to do that, he would first have to survive, like Tom, the boy he was reading about in *Tom Brown's School Days*.

Conrad wondered if he could pass his subjects? Algebra was tough. His nerves tensed. Would he make the first team ball club? In Bath Elementary School he had been king in sports. There could be no return.

A piercing whistle stopped the scrimmage for the morning gym period. Conrad jumped reflexively, but Rantsom laughed carelessly and said, "Come on, let's go read some spicy comics. We don't want to get bored."

They returned to class.

Six weeks later, Conrad read the gym bulletin posted in the study hall. He slumped in his seat and passed a sweaty palm over his upper lip, nerves ratcheting like a coiling spring.

Seeing the coach stride into the room, he only half heard him say, "Get down to work, class. Boys, don't be discouraged if you didn't make the varsity squad. Practice. Later, who knows?" His voice was oily and gushy, now.

"Psst! Congratulations, Rantsom. You're the only winner here. At least you made the second team." It was Eudora Ashley who sat just behind Conrad and whispered across the aisle to Rantsom. He could see Rantsom wrinkling up his face and shaking his head. His crew cut was unkempt.

"You didn't get cheerleader?" Rantsom asked.

"No. Politics got in the way. Dad lost a school-board race," she said. Her glossy brown hair draped her shoulders.

"Conrad, I do not see your name on the varsity listing. You were weak competition. That's why I'm only a second stringer now. And after six weeks of practice." He seemed menacing, saying, "Shave that upper lip will you? It looks like who knows what." Conrad was sensitive about his new black mustache.

"I'll ask Coach Roberts. Maybe it's a typo." Conrad knew it was a lame excuse. He had seen no Amberger, Conrad, posted on the bulletin board. Both he and Rantsom were just too skinny. A whirring pencil sharpener drilled at his nerves and he heard the crackle of papers over the room. He had failed to get on the basketball team and what about algebra? Would he be able to face his dad or the outside world?

The bell rang. Eudora walked the hallway with him to geography class. Floors cracked loudly under student traffic. Then, Conrad felt Eudora's hair touching his cheek. She leaned close and said, "I'm recruiting for the principal's string band. You play the guitar?" Eudora was enterprising and independent, always ready with a sunny smile.

"He's also organizing a fish and game club. The world must go on, Conrad."

"I learned acoustic guitar over the summer." Conrad envied Rantsom who could talk so easily to Eudora. Would Rantsom soon be asking her for a date? Conrad's thumping heart must not be heard!

"We'd like you to join the band, Conrad."

Still shocked, he said, "I'd love it." It was as if she had sensed his loneliness or known that the invitation would revive his withering soul.

"You know I'm friends with Tiffany and Steffany, Rantsom's older twin sisters, and often stay the night with them. Some coal camp kids have a chip on their shoulders, Conrad. Why?"

"Rantsom does for sure," he said. "He won't stay in school now that he only made the B team."

"He was caught spying on his sisters taking a bath," Eudora confided.

"He's hitting below the belt. That's foul play," he told her. "He's reading too many racy comics, too."

"The sisters call him Hot Shot," she said, and laughed heartily as they entered geography class. "I believe he's spoiled by his dad."

He hoped at some point she would admit despising Rantsom.

The first public band concert was scheduled for the middle of

November. But Conrad hurt his left wrist and splintered his Silvertone guitar in an automobile wreck the week before the concert. He was traveling to play on a local Saturday morning radio show. The wreck fractured his wrist and smashed up his new archtop guitar. His dad had lost control of their pickup truck on black ice. It flipped over twice, rolling down a steep embankment.

Rantsom said the auto accident was a lucky one, giving Conrad more time to learn his craft. He had been "weak competition" in basketball.

"You failed twice, Conrad," Rantsom flung at him.

"Rant, you need to learn banjo playing and join the band, to improve it."

"I'll do that."

Conrad thought of his graduation from high school. He remembered one day last summer when his grandmother had said to him, "Stick to your bush now." She always said that as she sent him out to pick blackberries. "Don't come back here with an empty bucket." Despite the boiling sun and prickly briars, he always filled that pail to the brim.

One day, in late December, Conrad hurried to the bus stop. He was running late because of reading well into the night. The stinging wind whipped his long black hair about and swished snow through nearby pine branches. He buttoned the collar of his denim jacket. A mile remained to be walked and during the night, six inches of snow had fallen. The roadway was slippery, slushy, with snow crunching under his boots.

Could the first semester be survived? His dad often spoke of their original ancestor, Conrad Johannes, sailing down the Rhine River, alone, to the New World. There was no return possible to Germany where he had been a dresser of grapevines; he could only survive as an indentured vintner, in Virginia, to Governor Spottswood, who had paid the ship's passage over the waters.

Conrad had failed in basketball, perhaps in math as well, and smashed his only guitar. One would have to be borrowed for the spring concert. Eudora's dad had bought her a new Martin; she agreed to lend him her older Kay guitar. Such excitement playing the concert and hearing that applause could never be forgotten. If only he did not have a failing report card.

During the entire first semester he had not asked even one girl for a date. Was that a failing grade, too?

His forehead ached from the cold, his nostrils stuck together.

He started running.

Conrad's Passage

Rantsom had been kicked off the second team recently for reading in class. Eudora said Mr. Sparks, who taught health, called on him, "Who pioneered in blood circulation?" Rantsom said, "It beats the hell out of me." The question had caught him by surprise; his head had been buried in an ever-present comic book.

Rantsom spoiled daily for a fight. Conrad felt that he must have dealt a severe blow to Rantsom's ego by slapping away the basketball during practice. The coach had paired them at guard.

The small bus stop building seemed deserted.

Approaching it past a cluster of bushes, a blinding, hissing ball of snow struck the back of Conrad's head! Without thinking, he pivoted on his left foot striking out with a right open palm; it smacked Rantsom's left jaw at the angle. He crumpled like a marionette, and lay silent in the deep snow, eyes glazed and smoky. "God! I've killed Rant," Conrad thought, horrified. "I only saw a blurry movement, not a boy."

Then, Rantsom started laughing! Or crying. What was happening?

Before Conrad could think, he grappled with Rantsom, pinning his arms; and, running with him firmly in his grip, he body-slammed him into the deep snow. Conrad did not know why he did that; it seemed as if an unknown passion gripped his hands!

Rantsom tried to laugh again, but choked. Conrad could find nothing to do to still his trembling hands. He rubbed them again and again up and down the front of his coat.

Rantsom snuffled and slowly crawled to his knees, his face dripping blood onto the snow. He was out of it. Conrad offered to lend a handkerchief. As he leaned over Rantsom, he realized that his own nose was bleeding, too. The droplets quickly balled up in the snow like a string of cinnamon beads.

As Conrad became aware of things, a car pulled to a stop. A neighbor, the school principal's sister, was offering them a ride to school in her new Chrysler New Yorker. They both crawled into the roomy back seat.

"Aren't you boys late?" Mrs. Cindy Combs asked. "What have you been doing to one another? I'll get you to school. Quick! Use these paper towels."

"Our faces are still bloody red!" Rantsom smirked, his blond crew cut disheveled and wet from melting snow and ice. Conrad saw the tiny gold hairs on Rantsom's smooth cheeks.

"I can't believe I hit someone," Conrad said in disbelief, and passed a cold hand over his numbing face.

"Hit! That was a mule kick, Conrad."
"Why were you late, Rantsom?"
"I intended to miss school today."

As they entered the old stone and glass building, Rantsom said, "See you around, Buddy," and walked rapidly away toward the bathroom.

Conrad had a two-week break between semesters.

A Christmas card from Eudora included a note. She had it from Rantsom's sisters that he had gone to Cincinnati to live with relatives, and play basketball there.

"Well, let him stalk those sidewalks for a while," Conrad thought. Wow! What a Christmas present.

His dad, Monroe, had talked to the school authorities about the fight and brought home Conrad's report card. Conrad had an A in science, a B in all other subjects, but a conditional in math. At least he had another chance there. He would "stick to his bush."

With Rantsom gone he would be in the string band with Eudora next semester, without competition. The way to graduation seemed clearer. And he would join the fish and game club, too. That meant a monthly meeting with the state wildlife management representative, Mr. Lon Reynolds, and a welcome break from classroom work! What fun to learn how to feed wild birds and how to safely hunt wild animals for food.

He felt himself relaxing, as if that coiled spring deep inside him had started unwinding and releasing its tension.

During the holidays, he finished reading *Tom Brown's School Days*. It seemed right for Tom to have to fight for survival at school, so why not himself? No need to regret that. Conrad's conscience eased. After all, his ancestor had had a legal fight for his freedom from the governor of Virginia.

Catching his dad and older brother out of the house, Conrad used his dad's gold plated razor to shave his dark moustache. While brushing on the warm, moist Old Spice shaving lather, he thought it smelled good enough to eat.

After shaving and cleaning the razor, as he had seen his dad do hundreds of times, he ran a hand over his rough, stubbly face, and felt manly.

Second Act

Jason Atkins

The smell of embalming fluid and stale cigarette smoke was heavy in the air of the workroom. No one else could stay for long in this room, but Gaines Twicegood was happy working here. That is, he was as happy as Gaines could be. At times, he regretted joining his brother Dewey as partner and licensed embalmer at Twicegoods Inc. Dewey talked him into attending mortician's school in 1964. For the last twenty years, this workroom had become, more and more, his only reason to leave his small apartment. He was good at his job; perhaps, one of the best in the business. His long, thin fingers would begin to work, moving first with the scalpel, then the pumps. Each educated digit moved with precision, from the scalpel to the plugs to the pumps, a continued flowing motion over to the ashtray and the burning cigarette. The combination of formaldehyde, smoke, and vodka created a chemical combination that turned Gaines's thick hair yellowish grey, matching his skin and eyes.

The other employees didn't like to be in the same room with Gaines. Especially was this true for Bob Doss. Bob was pick-up and delivery man. Tonight he delivered a new client at 8:30 p.m. It was late and Gaines had begun to relax early, with his evening vodka. This pick up was an intrusion into his mood. He didn't want to have to become professional this late at night. Recently, the company had purchased a new state-of-the-art body pick-up bag. General Electric had designed it with an electric body warmer and moisturizer. The salesman had guaranteed it to prevent the onset of rigor mortis up to thirty hours. This was only the second customer using the bag, so Gaines had his doubts. The shape of this bag indicated the corpse was in a sitting position. Gaines hadn't looked inside because he didn't want to disturb the disposable liner. He knew it would take extra work and skills to straighten the body. Irritated, he pushed Bob's call bell.

"Come over here, boy," Gaines said, "I want to know something. Who is this? What's the name? Where did you pick up the body?"

Bob saw the bag had not been opened and replied. "Hell, Gaines, I don't know who the guy was! A young guy, only had his pants on! He was bent like that and his neck was pulled and red when we put him in the bag."

"Where did you get him?" Gaines asked in a curious tone.

"At the city jail," Bob said. "He was on the floor of the isolation cell. The officers hadn't moved him." In the same breath without stopping, Bob asked, "What you think happened to a young guy like that, to bend him so stiff?"

"I don't know," Gaines said. "Better go find Dewey and send him in here. Tell him, 'I ain't doing nothing tonight, if I don't have to!'"

Gaines looked at the formaldehyde cooker. It was cold. He didn't want to force himself to work that night. This was especially true if there wasn't going to be an early viewing of the deceased. Dewey should know. He would wait on Dewey. The burning butt of the last cigarette furnished a new light to another unfiltered Chesterfield while he waited. The house phone rang. It was Dewey.

"What you want?" Dewey asked.

"This new pick up tonight, what about him?" Gaines asked.

Dewey responded, "What you mean? What about him?"

Gaines said, "I mean, dammit, who is he? What happened? Bob said he picked him up at the jail. He's stuck sitting down in the body bag. Does he have to be ready in the morning? Looks like I will have to use the straightening vise. That takes extra time! What's the story? Was he a cripple?"

"I don't know, Grimes," Dewey said. "His brother, Joe Fletcher, called me about five this afternoon. I know him from Rotary. There is some mix-up with the law and the funeral won't be for a few days. Wait till in the morning to work on him, uh-um, after I talked to his brother," Dewey continued. "I remembered something about this Allen Fletcher. Killed his wife about four months ago. It was in all the papers. They were a young couple. Can't remember a reason. Seems she was completely naked when he came home unexpected! She was supposed to have been at the college office. I'll find out more when I see Joe tomorrow. See you in the morning." Without waiting for an answer, Dewey hung up.

Gaines had all he needed to know, for now. He sighed, reached for the one-half gallon jug of Vodka, and poured himself a reward of three good fingers in a tall glass. He walked over to the lead sink and turned the water on. In one big gulp he killed the Vodka and filled the glass again with water for a chaser. Now, Gaines was happy, as happy as Gaines could be, for tonight. He glanced at the bent figure outlined in the new electric bag, continued looking around at the all blue ceiling and walls, then clicked the lamp off. Leaving, he thought, "Thank God for new technology and General Electric."

The workroom was dark and quiet now. The only occupant was what remained of Allen Fletcher. Allen was dreaming again. It was the same old dream that had haunted him since a small boy. He was able to fly; no one else knew. Just raise his arms like the wings of a bird, and he could soar over trees and houses. It was a joy, as a child, to raise his arms and rise above his playmates or family. There was power in the act, especially since he was shorter than most of the other kids. The dream continued into adulthood, always with new versions of this ability to fly. During the dream, he was always half conscious, knowing that it was only the same old dream. He would wake up! He always did, whenever he willed it. Tonight, the dream was a little different. He would float out and up into a bright golden light. The light was warm and like a beacon. It swirled around him, coating his flying body with golden mist. This mist moved in a pulling, magnetic motion, yet there was no breeze or draft. He could reverse flight downward to an area dominated by curling, soft blue haze.

It was the blue periods that produced his nightmares. There was no joy in being able to look down and see his own bent body on the jail floor. He thought, this is like a stage play and I am an actor. It was so real he could hear and understand the voices of the other characters in the melodrama. They were talking about him, just as if he wasn't there. The golden light held and drew him closer and closer. He could see them put his own body into a cloth bag. The riding motion to another location was felt. Blue mist became much stronger now! It was just at his feet before. Now it was around him completely, the same as blue fog. Looking down, he could see himself in the same bag completely wrapped in blue. He was on a table, a long table covered with tile. This was not the same as his other dreams! Before, he had always been able to will himself awake. He would wake up now. It wasn't a joy to fly anymore. The books had taught him to believe he could and he would do what he tried. Now, he was really giving it his best try. Still he could not wake himself. The golden mist, with the strong center light, became brighter. Its pull became more powerful. Again, he began to float and fly upward. Panic and terror began to dominate his thoughts! Even in dreams, he had been able to control his thoughts in the past. "So what's wrong with me," he anguished? Why, why am I losing my mind. Am I crazy?" No, he thought to himself! He would control this somehow! Hadn't he studied most of the control your own mind, self-help books. This positive attitude approach had helped him rise from the very wrong side of the tracks, in "Skaggs Hollow," to a respected citizen and business leader. Use it now, he thought! Use this positive mental attitude! He would break this nightmare with the power of his own mind and will!

The blue phase returned slowly. He could see the room plainly now. It was his body. It had to be real! Each instrument on the white cart next to his table was plainly visible. There was also some long device lying next to him. More like a steel pole, with cloth straps along the side. A small turnbuckle was located by each strap. At this moment, he knew he was in a mortuary. In the way the mind has of knowing, he accepted it was not a dream. He was dead! No, no, it can't be so! It couldn't be! Yet, still his mind just knew, his body was dead. Using every power of concentration of will, not a muscle would move. His confused, scrambled brain became quiet, panic left slowly. Acceptance began to creep into his soul. Slowly, too, the last traces of the bright golden light drifted out of his mind's eye. Now only the soft blue remained. The same voices he had been conscious of early began to speak near him. A door opened and he was aware of footsteps close by.

Gaines walked over to the work table with the drain troughs on each side. This morning, the bent figure in the bag was awaiting his skills. He pushed the electric button under the formaldehyde heater and then started to fill a small percolator from the sink tap. Coffee was stuffed tight into the top container and the pot was plugged in next to the embalming fluid heater. Gaines emptied the stale butts from two large glass ashtrays. Now, he had room to fill them again, this new morning. His wake-up tonic of one half orange juice and one half Vodka he had taken before leaving his apartment was beginning to clear his head. He checked the wheeled, white-enameled table close by. Laid out in rows were his trade tools, two sharp scalpels, one long steel tong, and then he added six orifice plugs of specially treated, hard cotton. Other than two curved surgical needles with pink silk thread, he was ready for work. The coffee aroma began to compete with the cigarette smoke for the air in the room. This was Gaines's ready-to-go signal. He slid the body bag and its occupant over onto the drain table. The zipper opened easily—along with the smaller zip on the inner lining. It was the first time he had seen the body. It looked good, still soft and workable.

Now, it was coffee time before the rubber gloves were pushed on. The cup he used was a big one, almost took the whole pot of coffee to fill it. Gaines always drank it black. The big cup handle would allow him to stop work and sip, even with the gloves on. Once a big slurp of coffee was down his throat, he began to work the outside bag off the body. It was difficult since the unnatural bend made it hard to slip off. Next, the disposable inner liner was slit with the scalpel and off it came. Gaines thought to himself, "This is a nice-looking young man." He remembered part of what Bob Doss had told him last night. No belt, not even socks—only a pair of khaki pants dressed the body. He reached for the scalpel to cut the pants to make them come off easier. Then, as always, he remembered what store the loved ones set by the clothes off of a corpse. Slowly, he forced the pants off and now, nude, the body was ready for straightening in the vise. Gaines lit another cigarette and took two long sips of the hot coffee. With his eyes, he began to measure his next step.

The minute Gaines had opened the bag, Allen had been aware of his every action. He could feel the transfer of his body and the slide of his pants. The awareness of the blue ceiling and walls was oppressive, but he could not move or speak. Once more, fear and panic began to stir in his brain. It was a turmoil, "Am I crazy," he thought, "Am I just dreaming? If I could only scream!" The golden mist began to swirl in again. This time, there was a strange comfort in the beginnings of the gold light's brightness. The light surrounded by this tunnel of gold became brighter than ever. "Let go! Let go!" an inner voice said. It was more comfortable than fighting the blue, he began to relax and drift upward.

Gaines felt the fluid tank and checked both electric pumps. Not quite warm enough to do a good flush job, he judged. The morning paper was still in a roll in his hip pocket. Standing by the table he opened the paper and spread it over the body to read. Because the body was on its left side facing Gaines, the bent waist made a good angle to hold the newspaper steady. Moving the big crock cup over next to the body, he began to read and smoke. There was no system to his reading. Just spread the paper and start with anything that caught his eye. The banner letters of one long article caught his attention immediately. He read on:

"Local Man Hangs Himself in City Jail" Allen Skaggs Fletcher, age 34, hanged himself sometime between one and two p.m. yesterday afternoon. Police Chief Jackson stated that Fletcher was in a padded isolation cell which was security checked every hour. As a safety measure, the prisoner had been allowed only his pants and shirt. There were no overhead fixtures or high bars in this cell. Chief Jackson stated that what Fletcher did was almost impossible. He was able to tie his shirt around his neck and secure it to a short horizontal bar on his cell wall. This bar was only three feet from the floor. By locking his body in a sitting position he was able to hang himself. The body was discovered during the 2 p.m. security check. The county coroner pronounced him dead at 3 p.m. and set the time of death 1½ hours earlier. Chief Jackson said he had never known of any prisoner with the willpower it took Fletcher to hang himself in a sitting position. Allen Fletcher was being held for the brutal stabbing and mutilation of his young wife in their fashionable Windsor Heights home.

Gaines looked up from the paper thinking, that explains why the body is in a sitting position. This man's will must have been strong. For the first time, he lifted the paper up and really looked at the body as a person. "Poor devil," he thought, "Wonder what his wife did?" Gaines was sympathetic. With three former wives himself, he never understood them but never thought he could kill one! The fluid was warm now. He dropped the paper on the floor, moved the coffee cup out of the way, and picked up the body-straightening vise. Not many occasions in his work was this vise necessary. Usually, he used it before the pumping. An impulse to embalm first struck Gaines. He propped the vise against the white side cart. The right arm of the body was on the up side. He picked up his short blade scalpel. Lifting the arm, he moved to the armpit with the blade point.

Allen was conscious of every move around him. There was a difference; he couldn't see his own body from a distance as before. The golden fog was gone, but the strong presence in the light seemed near. He knew the mortician was ready to stop his awareness forever.

The blade of the knife was cold against his armpit. Suddenly, an unexpected strong surge of survival flooded his consciousness. For the first time, during all this nightmare, he knew the golden presence was his salvation. A long pleading prayer flowed from his being. "Please, please, God, I repent; I am sorry! Please forgive me! Just give me one more chance to live!"

Gaines had just inserted the blade edge under the skin of the armpit. For no apparent reason, the body relaxed. The muscles, holding the sitting position, almost imperceptably began to straighten. This was so unusual it caused Gaines to pause. He placed the scalpel down and thought. "Dewey should see this." The bell button to Dewey's apartment was on the wall. He pushed this and waited for his brother.

Hearing the bell, Dewey knew it was some kind of emergency call. Pulling his pants on over his pajamas, he hurried down to the workroom. As soon as he opened the door, he knew something had happened by the expression on Gaines's face. He asked calmly, "What's up?"

Gaines pointed to the now relaxed body and said, "I believe this man is alive!" This was the first time Gaines had thought of Allen as anything but his trade term, "the body." Dewey walked over to the table and stood by his brother. Looking closely at Allen, he bent even closer to his face. "Gaines," he ordered, "call the life-saving crew at Riverside Hospital immediately. Be sure you put everything away before they get here!"

Gaines didn't expect this reaction from Dewey and bent over Allen's head to see what had created the quick decision. A large tear had rolled out of the corner of Allen's right eye. It had traveled across the bridge of his nose to join another twin tear from his left eye. They had formed the sea of life on Allen's cheek.

The Gardener

Terry Cox-Joseph

It began the first of March, when the garden center down the street opened for the season. Maryanne pulled her late model four-door into the gravel parking lot and homed in on a row of tiny green sprouts, lined up in little black plastic containers on a rustic outdoor table. She said the bright green chives were calling to her. Just a dollar each. She picked one up, cradled it in the palm of her hand, inhaled the faint scent, tucked it into the outside pocket of her purse, and took it home.

Over a cup of herbal tea made from the garden out back, she told me how she used a trowel that was left from the previous home-owner, gently lifted the soil, and lovingly inserted the chives into their new home.

"It was the strangest sensation," she whispered, as though someone else were listening. "It seemed like the trowel quivered in my hand, and I felt like I had to have that little trowel with me all the time. I couldn't stop thinking about it." She laughed and blushed, tossing her strawberry blonde curls over her shoulder like a schoolgirl.

On her next trip to the garden center, she bought an American redbud sapling. It was only two feet high, but the leaves were round and full and cheerful. She described how she stroked the leaves, felt their softness, admired their openness. She had to have the redbud.

She placed it carefully on the floor of her car, cradled it with crushed newspaper, and brought it home, where she dug a larger hole than the one she'd dug for the chives, this time in the front yard. She described how she loosened the soil, weeded a bit, squeezed the pot from the sides, then watched the soil gently crumble as she removed the rootball.

Looking back on it, I should have never purchased a small container of lavender for her just after they moved in. The lavender was only fifty cents, and I remember seeing her husband ascend the front steps the day before with his arms filled with roses. "Our anniversary!" he shouted over the fence, which gave me the perfect excuse to get a housewarming gift and introduce myself.

Maryanne exuded thanks with more enthusiasm than such a tiny gift warranted, and immediately planted the lavender a few feet away from the chives.

Each morning, after seeing the kids onto the school bus, she'd water her new herbs and redbud, singing to herself. Or was she talking to the flora? None of the words held any meaning for me, gibberish, or some foreign language that I couldn't quite catch from my kitchen window. I watched her till the rows with a hoe and a spade, as though she were preparing for a large influx of agricultural crops. Tenderly, she mingled perlite and sand with deep, black topsoil, amending the hard red clay from below, caressing the surface as though stroking the face of a beloved child.

Sometime in April, when I returned home from a day of errands, she'd filled in the empty rows of soil near the lavender and chives with sage, rosemary, spearmint, peppermint, pineapple mint, chocolate mint, and lemon balm. The mints especially seemed to be growing at an alarming rate, even as I stared. I worried that they would spread into my yard—not that I disliked herbs, but mint could take over if you didn't keep it in check. And I felt as though there was some complicity on my part, for having bought Maryanne the lavender.

But there were worse things than invasive mint. It was better than crabgrass or kudzu, I rationalized. Then she planted a Mexican fan palm about ten feet away from the redbud in the front. Strange bedfellows, but it was her yard.

What really caught my attention was the day she drove home in a new Ford pickup, fire-engine red. She'd traded in her four-door sedan so she could bring things home from the nursery.

Her first load was five yards of cedar mulch. She stood on the back of the truck, rear door flat open, and pitched hunks of mulch like a farmer. The pitchfork was yellow and seemed to glow, even in the afternoon sun. I shouted to her over the fence, invited her to come sit on my porch when she was finished, to share some iced tea, but she just mopped her brow, smiled and said she'd have to greet the kids when they got off the bus.

"Some other time, then," I shouted. Some childish part of me felt a nudge of anger and envy that she was more interested in her yard than real people. It was ridiculous. It wasn't as though we were best friends. But we could have been. I liked her. She was enthusiastic, cheerful, and obviously hardworking. She had a wholesome, down-to-earth attitude that appealed to me. But her kids were still in school, while mine were grown, and I had to admit we were at different points in our lives.

Soon after, she planted fountain grass in great quantities, spikes and puffs circling the redbud tree like happy dancers. Which was entirely appropriate for May Day.

What wasn't appropriate was the half-dozen upright elephant ears, the Washington Hawthorne, the deodar cedar, the snowball viburnum, and the Japanese black pine. She was getting a bit obsessive and I wanted to say something to her. I just couldn't make sense of it any more. How would the plants and trees get enough sunlight? What about the differing moisture needs? She only had a quarter of an acre split between front and back, so while the back yard was filled with herbs, spices, and garden flowers, the front was wall-to-wall jungle. On an eighth of an acre, I would have planted a redbud tree and a couple of azaleas, placed geranium-filled pots on either side of the front door, and called it a day. In fact, that's very much what my yard looked like.

I went away for a few days to tend to my sick father, and I returned in the middle of a downpour. Even with the wipers set to the fastest speed I couldn't see clearly through the windshield. It was everything I could do just to creep into the driveway safely, pop open my umbrella, and race into the house.

When the rain let up a few days later, Maryanne's yard had flourished beyond all recognition. Now, when her kids got off the bus, I could no longer see them run all the way to the front door; their path was obscured from my vision by the redbud, the Japanese black pine, the Mexican fan palm, and what appeared to be an entire jungle of bamboo. Why in heaven's name had she planted bamboo? It was so invasive. And here I'd been worried about the mint creeping over to my yard. Still, I had to admit it was lush, and filled the void where just a few short months ago, her little brick house had been centered on an otherwise unremarkable parcel of land. She knew what she was doing. Half of anything I'd ever planted had always died.

I ran into her in mid-summer at the garden center, which was certainly no surprise. What was strange was the murmuring coming from the rhododendrons, a cascade of voices, whispering, tumbling over one another, skipping from leaf to leaf, pale peach bloom to vermilion bloom to quivering white bloom. Or perhaps it was just

Maryanne talking to them, a habit she'd exercised more frequently as her landscaping collection grew.

After a year, Maryanne ran out of space in her yard. There was simply no place to plant anything else. I debated whether I should stop by and politely suggest she not attempt to plant anything else. But every time I'd asked her to tea she was too busy, and I couldn't very well just ring the doorbell and blurt my opinions into her face. It had gotten to the point where she barely waved any more. Maybe I was a pest. A nosy neighbor. I didn't want to be in her way.

Besides, there was something daunting about treading on her property now, something almost possessive. I just didn't feel right traipsing over there, barging into her paradise, and forcing my style on her. She probably thought my conservative taste was boring, anyway.

But I missed her. And I missed the chance to get to know her better. I needed to be more assertive. Stop internalizing and start doing. I decided to call her, and on the third ring, Bert picked up and told me that Maryanne was outside in the yard. Of course. Even though it was dark, she was working under the bright glare and deep shadows cast by the floodlight.

He promised to have her return my call.

I phoned twice after that, and she finally returned my call two weeks later. She was out of breath, and I felt that just taking the time to talk to me was an inconvenience, a misuse of time in an over-burdened calendar. Obviously, my landscaping opinion would be of no use to her. Funny, how just hearing her voice and running into her constant stream of landscaping excuses had started to make me feel sorry for myself, to the point of becoming depressed. I mean, she talked to her plants, for heaven's sake, and she didn't have time to talk to me. She said everything was fine, and added, "Everyone is growing, growing, growing! Oh, just growing." The way the words rasped from her throat, it was as though she were speaking of a lover, tones hushed, velvety and coarse at the same time, too private to discuss in public, too exciting to go unsaid.

That was the last time I spoke with her. I tried to put her out of my mind. Clearly, she was too busy and I was wasting my time. I threw myself into researching my family ancestry on the Internet, painting the dining room, and preparing for my monthly book club. So seldom did I think of her that I was amazed to see her a month later, pacing back and forth in front of her house, way in front of her house, by the curb, pacing like a caged wolf, a container of gold daylilies in her hand. I burst out laughing at the absurdity of it. There was absolutely no place else to plant anything. I could sense her agitation and frustration through the car windows as I drove by. It was an almost imperceptible tingling, an agitation that zinged into my brain and forced the smile from my face. I drove on, parked the car, and turned my back. I didn't need her wolfish pacing in my life.

The next day, I passed by her on my morning walk. "Hi," was all I managed to say, knowing she wouldn't respond. By then my anger had waned, and I pitied her, despite the fact I knew that she was happy, squatting over the front curb, spade in hand, tresses tied back in a '40s style bandanna, legs sturdy in khaki shorts and hiking boots, planting daylilies along the sidewalk. I'd been convinced there was no space left to plant anything, but it seemed as though the yard had somehow grown to meet the capacity, as though it had stretched in some inexplicable way. That space hadn't been there before. I was sure of it. I walked briskly away, determined not to look back.

I casually mentioned to another neighbor that Maryanne seemed to have taken over the yard with new plants, rather, the yard had overtaken her, and the neighbor exclaimed, "There's a house in there?" Just the exclamation, the tone of his voice, made me laugh, but more than that, it validated my perception.

And then Bert called, only the second time he had ever called me, the first time asking us to take in the newspapers while they were out of town for a weekend, months back. He said that he and Maryanne were divorcing. I had to sit down. It felt as though my stomach had caved in. Not Bert and Maryanne. So young—just in their thirties—and the kids still in elementary school. What happened?

In a husky, choked voice, Bert told me that Maryanne had ignored the family, stopped making meals, never supervised the kids' homework, refused to dine out with other couples, and had quit her job, all to take care of the yard.

"'It can take care of itself!' I'd told her, and it was like she turned into an alien or something," he said. "She just couldn't hear me, refused to stop buying more plants and trees, had charged up a double-digit credit-card debt in gardening and landscaping supplies. I begged her to go to counseling, she wouldn't hear any of it."

And then the plants started coming into the house. She wasn't buying hanging planters, philodendrons, windowsill African violets. The outdoor plants were actually growing into the house.

"I was taking a shower last week and I noticed a vine creeping through the drain," he said. "Kind of gave me the creeps, you know? And then the power kept flicking on and off, really messing with my computer. Next thing I knew, Building Codes was knocking at the door, telling us the house would have to be torn down."

I felt nauseous. The hair on my arms stood on end. My head began to spin. Involuntarily, I glanced over my shoulder at my own philodendron, twining lazily from its white basket, tickling the windowsill.

"Where is Maryanne?" I managed to whisper.

"She's rented an apartment in Midtown," he said.

I hope she'll be all right, I thought, but didn't dare say aloud. It seemed disrespectful for some odd reason, like walking on a dead person's grave. I knew that if I was thinking about her, I would have to visit her. And if I visited her, I might get too involved. But how could I not reach out to her?

As the days shortened and the shadows stretched into autumn, I found every excuse not to visit. Committee meetings, work, errands, meals to cook. Let sleeping dogs lie, my grandmother always said. All those months tried so hard to be her friend, and now, I was the one making excuses to avoid her. Not that she knew what I was thinking. But somehow, it felt that way.

The morning before Labor Day, I awoke to a roar so loud, vibrations so fierce, I thought it would take my house down. I lay in bed for a few seconds, clutching the sheets and trying to discern the direction of the sound, but a crash shook my bedroom window. I yanked the cord to the Venetian blinds and realized that it was the scraping and thumping of a backhoe. I recognized the city logo on the side of the vehicle and understood that it was destroying Maryanne's sweet little red brick house, which was trembling and crumbling beneath the force of metal teeth and rubber treads. With each shingle that fell and piece of wooden framing that cracked, a whining moan arose, like a million voices grieving. With a great shudder, Maryanne's house caved in, and a cloud of dust rose upward in supplication. Fat yellow-green canes of bamboo groaned under the weight of the backhoe, rhododendrons quaked and shuddered. When the American redbud snapped in two, I heard a scream rise up to the clouds. I couldn't be certain if it wasn't my own voice. But I couldn't be certain it wasn't the redbud, either.

When the last of the house and yard was piled into an industrial-sized waste container and hauled away, a shimmer of heat rose up from the property, formed an iridescent cloud, hovered for a moment, and floated away.

I felt as though a part of me had died. Too weak to stand, I lay on the couch and let sleep overtake me. I spent the entire day and all the next night on the couch, arising with an urgent need to visit Maryanne.

I found her address where I'd written it when Bert had called with the news. Just picking up the pad gave me a chill, as though someone had poured shaved ice down the back of my sweater. I shook off the feeling, tucked the note into my pocket, and started out for her apartment. I wondered if she'd be angry with me for not being more supportive. I debated stopping by the grocery store and picking up a card. I wondered if I should pick up a bouquet. And then an idea hit me—why not give her a little housewarming gift just like I'd given her before, something small but thoughtful. Without a real yard, she would be cramped, but without a real yard, she would be bereft.

She would need something to remind her of the outdoors. I drove up to the garden center, the gravel clicking beneath my tires, and I knew exactly what I would buy: A miniature pumpkin gourd, perfectly in tune with the season and small enough for an apartment. She could set it right on the windowsill.

I purchased the gourd and walked briskly to the car. The need to see her, to make sure she was all right, to know, now, sent my heart and mind racing as though I'd downed an entire pot of coffee. Sweat built up on my forehead and palms, and I lost my grip on the wheel twice. I blotted my palms with a tissue and turned on the air conditioning, even though it was easily fifty outside. Stupid hot flashes.

The building was brick with white clapboard accents, somewhat Colonial in appearance. I'd driven by these apartments before but had never really noticed them. Nondescript and set back from the street, they were fronted by a blacktop parking lot edged with scraggly shrubs and patches of dry dirt.

Hers was the first apartment next to the management office. I used the knocker gently, afraid I would startle her, and the single clack echoed through the long hall. I heard her light footsteps, and with my throat tight and my stomach in a lump, I waited.

There was Maryanne, as cute as I remembered, freckles dancing about her cheeks, smile as wide as a sunflower.

"Look who's here!" she exclaimed, and threw her arms around me. "Come in, come in! Have some tea!"

My trepidation drained away with each sip, crisp and clear against my throat. Maryanne pushed a small plate of vanilla wafers toward me and it was hard to resist them. I ended up eating them all.

She asked me about book club, then told me how her kids were doing in school, as though nothing out of the ordinary had happened to bring her to this place, this plain little apartment with plain carpet and plain cupboards.

As I glanced around the kitchen, I admired how perky the miniature gourd looked over the kitchen sink, a shaft of sunlight intersecting its center, and I wished I were a painter so I could capture its simple beauty.

We finished an entire pot of tea, and, totally convinced that Maryanne was safe and happy and stable, that she was going to make it on her own, I paused for one last hug in the open doorway. As I inhaled the vague scent of shampoo from her copper curls, another, crisper, more biting scent took its place. Chives—there, on the kitchen windowsill, beside the pumpkin gourd which moments ago had sat alone, striped in sunlight like a painting. Next to them, through a crack in the open window, whimsical vines waved in the breeze, reaching tendrils across the sill, seeking a hold.

I blinked and took a step away from Maryanne, and as I backed out into the hallway, I distinctly heard the sound of voices, chittering in the sun.

The Day a Crow Snatched My Baby Sister

Pete Freas

You kids are sitting here griping about the heat and bugs and everything. When I was your age, we didn't have air conditioning. Nobody did. We opened windows and sat on the porch, talking with neighbors when they walked past, and read until it got too dark outside. We didn't have TV . . . or video games either. But we had a radio, and we listened to it. Later, after we moved out of the city and we became teenagers, we got a TV, but we still listened to rock'n roll on the radio when we did our homework.

Summertime, we sat on the porch a lot. We knew all our neighbors, and we couldn't get away with anything because someone always knew who we were and would tell our parents what we'd been doing, and then we'd be in trouble. The only time we came inside was to eat or to go to bed, unless it was raining or it was winter. Nowadays everybody has air conditioning, and nobody knows who their neighbors are. No one even talks to neighbors.

These days, you worry about bugs and bees and the heat, and you don't want to go outside. That's a pity. Shoot, back then, we had ants the size of my dad's shoes. One time, when he had to replace one of the concrete steps up to the porch, he sprinkled some sugar and got some twenty or thirty ants to help him move this great big cement-slab step that must have weighed a couple hundred pounds. With them ants tuggin' and liftin' and pullin', he got the old, crumbly step out and the new one in place in no time at all. And that's the truth.

You kids today are afraid of bees! Why, we had honeybees the size of a small dog . . . like Scottie. That dog was something else—never stopped barking and yapping. My goodness, he yapped in his sleep chasin' rabbits or whatever. He'd even yelp while he ate. And eat! That dog'd snarf down a meal in three bites; sounded like he was attacking a bear.

Anyway, first time I saw the bees, Scottie was out on the narrow grass strip between the house and the sidewalk, and he started in to barkin' like when Gramps and Gram came, but there wasn't any car. I heard a loud hum that came through Scottie's barking, kind of like the background hum of a bagpipe. Then I saw the honeybee. She was as big as Scottie himself. Remember now, I only saw ants the size of my dad's shoes and this bee as big as Scottie; I had no idea bugs were supposed to be LITTLE. In fact, lots of people used to compliment my mother for her sunflowers; she would just smile and say, "Thank you," even though they were really just daisies! It was just the way things were when I was a "pup," as Gramps would call me.

So there I was staring at this big ol' bee while Scottie was barking his fool head off. When Mom came out and saw me pointing at the bee, she smiled and said, "Oh, a honeybee." She asked if I wanted to put out a bowl of sugar water for her and showed me how to dissolve a teaspoon of sugar in a small cereal bowl of lukewarm water. We laid it on the stone porch rail. That honeybee slowly hovered over to the stone rail and stuck out its tongue and sucked up all that sugar water like through a straw. The hum was kind of soothing.

That same afternoon the bee returned with a few of her friends, and we put out a bucket of sugar water for them. Next day she was back with a whole swarm of 'em. Mom put out another bucket for them, but this time in the back yard where there was more room and a little more privacy, even though the houses were crowded together in the city. Every morning and every afternoon after that, we put out a bucket of sugar water for the bees. They didn't come every day, but you always knew when they came to feed because it sounded like a lot of airplanes were flying around the house (there were no jets back then, just propeller planes, so there was no jet noise, just the loud, powerful "thrum" like at the race track my dad took us to a couple times out in the country).

I liked the bees. I loved to hear them come to feed and to watch them suck up all that sweet water. Sometimes we'd leave Kool-Aid; they liked lemon the best. Mom would leave a couple of empty jars out once a week, and after they had left, the jars were full of honey. Once I peeked through the curtain and saw just one bee fill a whole peanut butter jar.

Now in 1950, my baby sister was just a new-born infant. We would sit out on the porch, and people goin' by would all have to stop and come up on the porch and ogle her. You know, they'd "oooooh" and "ahhhhhh" and make stupid baby talk at her. Boy, the most proper people in the whole world make the most absolute fools of themselves in front of babies, even in public places.

We'd be sitting out there on the porch readin' or talkin' or daydreamin' or whatever, and Sis would be in Mom's lap or just on a blanket surrounded by rolled-up towels and pillow-cushions so's she wouldn't roll out onto the cement or down the steps or something. Some one of us was ALWAYS there, usually Mom or Dad, if not both of 'em.

This one particular day—I think Sis was maybe two weeks old or something like that—Mom had gone inside to get something to sew, I guess, and left me to keep an eye on Sis. Suddenly I heard this loud FLOP FLOP FLOP FLOP FLOP at the porch rail, and I turned around to see what it was. There was this huge crow as big in the body as me (not unusual, remember, because the wrens and sparrows were as big as a grown cat)! His wings had to be five feet long, each—a ten-foot span across. I thought, *Wow! Wouldn't it be cool to have big wings like that? I could fly around the school yard and swoop down on Barny Fernwater and peck him on the head 'cause he was always such a bully.* I don't know, maybe they'd get in the way more often than not. I sure woulda liked to have wings though. He alighted on the cement rail between the stone columns that held up the roof. I just stared, my mouth open in amazement. Scottie was barkin' and runnin' back and forth and barkin' and barkin'.

I didn't know about Good and Evil ("good" and "bad" was something else again), but I felt this chill and knew right down to my bones that I was looking at the face of Evil itself. That ol' black crow just stared at me and then hopped down next to my baby sister and turned his head to look down on her, lyin' there in her diaper on the blanket surrounded by cushions and rolled towels. At one and the same time, he hopped on top of her, wrapping his long, bony toes around her, and I leapt toward both of them.

He was already flapping them big ol' wings of his, tryin' to get flyin', but I'd grabbed both hands around one of his legs. His wings was beatin' on me and on the cement porch, and I was screamin' for Ma, and Sis was sleepin' through it all like without a care in the world. All that floppin' and wing-flappin' was draggin' me and Sis to the edge of those eight cement steps down to the sidewalk. I don't mind tellin' you, I was scared out of my wits. Just me and the crow floppin' and flappin' and screamin' and hollerin,' and baby sister sleepin,' and nobody to help out. Scottie was just adding to the commotion, darting in and out at us and barkin' and yappin'.

Then, all of a sudden, I felt intense heat, and all the flappin' stopped for just a moment. Even Scottie stopped barking. I looked up

The Day a Crow Snatched My Baby Sister

at the door and saw Mom standin' there just starin' at that crow. I ain't never seen her look like that before—nor since then either. Her eyes were red like two little fire pits; it was like she looked two laser beams of red light into that ol' crow (nobody knew about laser in those days, but I think Mom had it). She reached out next to her and seized the broom beside the door and swung it like a battle axe at that crow. The crow let go of Sis, and I let go of his leg; but Mom caught him a good lick with the broom and bounced him on his back down all eight of them steps to the sidewalk.

He lay stunned on the sidewalk for a moment, then flopped over and stood glowering back at Mom. Now birds aren't supposed to be able to show feelings in their expressions, but that crow radiated hate. His eyes gazed red right back at her two little laser eyes, and he just looked as if he was about to go at her when I heard this great, deep thrumming like bombers on a raid over Germany in the war. The crow turned his head and his appearance changed instantly from hateful to terrified, and he leapt into the air and flew across the street and up over the house there with a cloud of big ol' honeybees in hot pursuit.

One of the bees left the swarm and came back to the porch and stopped, and hovered above the very center of the top step, and looked at Mom, then at me, and then at Sis, who was now waking up, still on the blanket dragged along with us in our battle with the crow. Mom scooped both of us up in her arms, and we just stood there looking at the honeybee. I declare, I saw that bee smile. Scientists will tell you bees don't have the physical apparatus to smile or frown or make facial expressions. But I know what I saw. And the bee kind of glowed—there was a fan of light, a complete circle around that bee, kinda like a halo around the moon on a cool, damp night; and I felt very comfortable and safe. Then the bee turned and flew off after the swarm and that crow.

Man, them bees. How about that? We had our own swarm of "Watch Bees." Wow. I don't know about that ol' crow, but he sure was hateful and ugly, and fascinating in the way you can't stop staring at something awful that you don't want to see, but you just can't stop lookin'. You know?

That was some time ago; but, I can remember it just like it was yesterday. I mean, you don't forget something like that. Everything's different today though. Everybody's got air conditioning, and no one sits out on their porch or knows their neighbors. And honeybees are just little things any more—the size of marbles. I still love 'em; and I still eat a lot of honey.

Be glad you got air conditioning and TV and all that, I guess. Things just aren't the same any more. And if you find you got a bee hive like a big gray papier-maché ball, sort of Chinese-lantern lookin' thing, hangin' from a low branch of the tree outside your bedroom window, put out a bucket of sugar water for 'em. They're probably hornets (in that kind of nest), but you never know—they might be friends. So be nice to 'em. Even if they're no bigger'n a peanut, if you need 'em to chase off some bully, they might turn out to be your friends anyway.

I used to have a feather from that ol' crow's tail. I pulled it out of the broom Mom hit 'im with. I'd show it to you, but Mom made me burn it. Said it was nasty, and she didn't want it hangin' around the house causin' trouble. If you maybe don't believe any of this, I don't blame you. I wouldn't believe it either if I hadn't heard it from my own lips. Well, go on now, and be nice to them bees. It never hurts to have someone lookin' out after you. Go have some fun, and behave yourself.

The Door of Randolph Manor

Stephanie Friar

Mr. James Randolph stood in the library, looking out the window at the dreary English sky. He thought it rather ironic that there was a storm on the horizon; it suited his mood as his guests would soon be arriving. He wasn't looking forward to the meeting. His grandfather, the Earl of Aimsleigh had an agenda, which included one of the guests.

He took a sip of his tea and wondered how he was to deal with the situation. To his relief, the door opened behind him and he turned to find Alton, the butler, standing in the doorway. "What is it, Alton?" The man took a few steps into the room. "You wanted to know when the guests arrived, Sir. The carriage has just pulled through the gate; it will be here within minutes." James nodded. "Thank you Alton, I will greet our guests." He moved forward. "I am sure you have a great many things to do." The older man bowed and left the room. James moved through the door toward the hallway. He heard the carriage pull to a halt and spotted the women.

Allison Rankin swept through the door of Randolph Manor with her bright, apple-green, silk day dress and ivory, silk Spencer Jacket with green trim on the collar and sleeves. He knew it was Allison from the description his mother had given him. She looked around as she entered and seemed surprised that there was no one to greet them in the hallway. Allison stopped abruptly, causing her companion, following close behind, to stumble into her. She turned and glared at the young woman. "Good Heavens, watch what you are doing!" James frowned at the harsh tone as she spoke.

His mother and father had married for love, and they wanted the same for their son. Their grandfathers were close friends and had wanted the alliance of the families through their own children but the generation was all males and thus the task now fell on James.

He stepped back, further out of sight, and watched the lady pull off her gloves and bonnet. "Honestly, it baffles me at times how we are of the same lineage with you being so awkward." James watched as Allison squared her shoulders and looked down her nose at the other woman. She lifted the sides of her mouth as if to smile but she was too tight-lipped. "If you do anything to embarrass our family while we are here, I will never forgive you and I will make sure that you never come out in society again as long as I live. Do I make myself clear?" The younger woman nodded. James could not see the other woman's face and wondered why she took the abuse that Allison so obviously enjoyed inflicting upon her.

A carriage rambled up the park and stopped at the front door. James was at a disadvantage and could not see who it was, but hoped it was Brentwood, his closest friend. Roland Brentwood was a school chum and close neighbor. When James had asked him to come for the week he laughed and wanted to know who the woman was he would be running from. After he told Brentwood the plight he was in and the name of the woman, Brentwood grimaced at him but finally agreed to come and help him out.

Allison jerked the girl out of the doorway by pulling on her arm and the girl's bonnet flew off. Allison rolled her eyes as the woman bent to pick it up. "Hurry up!" The words were spat out in a harsh whisper and he suddenly got a glimpse of the other woman's profile. He smiled to himself. If she was some relation to Allison Rankin he couldn't see the resemblance.

Brentwood walked through the open door and gazed on Allison with some disdain. He had met Allison several times in town, and he would not wish his friend such an ill-conceived marriage.

"Brentwood." Allison smiled brightly up at him and curtseyed. Brentwood forced a smile and turned to the other woman and gave her a genuine smile. "Carson." He held out his hands and she came into his embrace. She kissed his cheek and when he released her he was still smiling. She does not look like Brentwood's type, James thought to himself as he listened intently to what was being said.

"How have you been?" She asked as she looked up at Brentwood. He needed to find out who this woman kissing his friend was and why had he not met her.

"Brentwood, I didn't hear you arrive." James stepped out of the doorway he had been hiding behind and walked toward the other man. They shook hands and he nodded to the ladies.

"I arrived a moment ago. Have you met your other guests?" James glanced between the women. "No, I thought perhaps they had come with you." Brentwood chucked. "Hardly, this is Miss Allison Rankin," he stated dryly as Allison dropped into a perfect curtsey and gave him a bright smile. "It's a pleasure to make your acquaintance, Mr. Randolph. I have heard much about you." He smiled as he studied her up close. She was tall and willowy. She had blond curls with bright blue eyes. Her lips were thin and she had a long straight nose. She was pretty but not someone that would catch James's attention.

"And I about you, Miss Rankin," he finally said, then turned to the other lady and smiled. Brentwood continued," This is Miss Carson Wrentworth. Her father is my uncle, my mother's brother, Captain Wrentworth. She has lived with her aunt since her mother died six years ago." As he studied the girl's face, James smiled. She was short and shapely, much like Brentwood's mother. She had auburn curls like Brentwood, but her eyes were a bright green and he felt that he could easily get lost in them. Her full lips were a natural wine color and she had just a hint of pink in her cheeks. A few freckles were scattered across her nose and cheeks, but they were lovely. He swallowed the lump that rose in his throat as he looked at her beautiful face.

"I believe we played together as children at Brentwood's estate," she said with a smile that reached her eyes and made them twinkle. He smiled at the sudden remembrance of their childhood antics but sobered quickly as he saw her pink cheeks turn a deeper red. He knew exactly what she was thinking because he was remembering it too. Brentwood chuckled at them both. "We were quiet a foursome, were we not?"

James cleared his throat and tried not to smile at Brentwood. He had enjoyed those times at his friend's estate—playing war and rescuing the damsel in distress.

"Who was the fourth?" Allison asked, braking into James's thoughts. He looked over at her only to receive an award-winning smile that he knew was less than sincere.

"My sister, Caroline; she was lately married to a Lord Cummings of Forest Hill in Yorkshire." She nodded with a lift of her brow. "Indeed, how fortunate."

"Yes indeed." Brentwood said dryly, as he stared at Allison and her fake smile.

"I would like to go to my room." She smiled up at Brentwood and then looked at James. "I am sure Carson would agree that we need to freshen up and change for dinner."

"Indeed, Miss Rankin. I will have Alton show you the way." He turned to the butler who was standing nearby. "Alton." The man bowed and motioned them to follow.

"Until this evening, Mr. Randolph." He simply smiled at Allison but reached for Carson's hand. "Miss Wrentworth." He kissed it lightly as she blushed and looked away. He caught the glare that Allison gave her cousin as she reached the stairs and he frowned.

Carson was gentle by nature, much like James's mother and would make him a fine wife, but how would he get rid of Allison Rankin in order to court Carson? He smiled as he remembered the last time they had played together at Brentwood's. He never would have imagined feeling like this after all these years, but he did. He glanced over at his friend who was studying him.

"It's Allison your family wants you to marry, not Carson. You need to remember that."

James replied, "I don't have to marry Allison if I choose not to, but it would please my grandparents." He smiled reflectively. "Do you remember when we were children? Everything seemed much simpler back then." Brentwood chuckled. "You mean when you would catch Carson in the maze and kiss her? Sometimes I think she would let you catch her just so she could kiss you." James smiled. "I'm sure of it." Both men laughed as they headed upstairs.

Carson Wrentworth was from two fine families, but her father was the second son and did not inherit a title. Her mother was the youngest child of the Elliot family. Although all of her sisters had married quite advantageously, her mother never had a good prospect of marrying well. She had married for love.

Carson lay across the bed and looked up at the tester of bright green and cream silk. The curtains were of the same silk, as was the bedding. She knew that the Randolphs were wealthy and she also knew that this was the reason Allison was willing to marry James Randolph. That is if he would have her. He didn't seem too impressed with Allison; in fact, he had paid more attention to her than Allison. Carson giggled to herself.

Allison had no trouble attracting men, it was keeping them that was the problem. She had the worst attitude of anyone Carson had ever met. Her parents spoiled her excessively and Jamie was Allison's last hope. Carson felt sorry for her. She had tried to be kind and helpful, but the older Allison got, the worse she became, and even harder to live with.

The Door of Randolph Manor

Carson closed her eyes and sighed. The image of James Randolph came to mind. He was tall and handsome with his caramel-colored eyes and sandy brown hair. He had broad shoulders and from the cut of his tailored clothes had very muscular arms and powerful thighs. His square chin held just the slightest hint of a clef, and his full lips were beautiful. She sobered and rolled onto her side. If I'm lucky, I will marry a merchant or a sailor. Lord James Randolph will not look at me twice. He would never want such a petite, shapely wife.

Carson wore a rose-colored silk dress with a high waist and square neckline. It flowed over her slippers made out of the same material. Her father provided her a clothing allowance, and she was pleased to receive so much from his generosity. However, when she went shopping, she always had to go with Allison, and if she even looked at a fabric twice, Allison would pick it up and keep it for herself. If she truly liked a fabric, Allison would insist on getting a dress made only for herself from the fabric. Carson was used to getting Allison's hand-me-downs in everything; when they went shopping, when they went out in public, and even with her men. All except for Brentwood of course since they were so closely related. Most men seemed to look at Allison's beauty but were always more pleased with Carson's personality and gentleness.

She sighed as she glanced at herself one last time in the looking glass. She had always felt that one day Jamie would come to London and sweep her off her feet. But when she found out that Allison was to marry him, her heart was broken and her dream shattered. The knight on a white horse coming to rescue her from the fire-breathing dragon named Allison disappeared. Now she would have to suffer through the constant flirting and cooing of Allison's forked tongue. She closed her eyes and tried her best to fight the urge not to run madly away. At times like these she missed her mother and father terribly. Maybe she would go and stay with her aunt Aggie while she was in the neighborhood. Brentwood would gladly take her to visit just to get away from Allison himself.

She squared her shoulders and headed across the hall to see if "Allison the Dragon" was ready for dinner. When she stepped close to the door she could hear Allison yelling at Millie, her maid. She must be having a bad time of it.

She took a deep breath and entered the room. "Are we ready?"

Allison glared at her. She was still wearing her dressing gown and her hair was hanging down around her waist. "Do I look ready?"

Carson forced a smile. "You look like you're ready for bed. What is the trouble?"

"I did not like the way she arranged my hair. Will you please help me?" Carson sighed. At least she said please. "Yes, please sit down." Allison did as she was told and held up a handful of pins.

"You didn't tell me you knew Mr. Randolph."

"It does not matter."

"Why were you blushing in his presence?"

"I wasn't blushing. We are old friends, though we have not seen each other in a very long time."

"Brentwood can easily sway him to not want me."

"And?"

"Will you talk to Brentwood and tell him to be nice?"

"Why don't you?"

"Because, it's still a little awkward between us."

"Do you still love him?"

Allison looked at Carson in the mirror.

"It doesn't matter. He despises me."

Carson saw the hurt Allison had in her eyes. "Maybe you should talk to him. He is more at ease in the country."

"I know that something happened, but I just do not know what!"

"Maybe he heard about your arranged marriage, and he didn't want to hurt Jamie. They have been close friends since they were young children."

Allison turned and looked up at Carson. "Do you think that he found out somehow?"

"Maybe, I can't say for sure. Brent would not talk to me about it, remember?"

"Yes, I remember." She looked down then got back into position so that Carson could finish pulling up her hair. They were quiet for a time, both women lost in their own thoughts.

"Carson?"

"What?" she said as she continued to work on Allison's hair.

"Is Mr. Randolph the man you were in love with from childhood?"

Carson looked up from her job and her hand stilled. "Why would you think that?"

"You spent a great deal of time here when you were a child."

"No, Jamie is just a friend." She averted her eyes and began pinning hair again.

When she put the last pin in, she stepped back and inspected her handiwork. "It's lovely as usual," Allison said with a hint of her attitude in her voice.

Carson loved Allison when she was herself and it was those rare moments when she cherished her cousin the most. "I'm going to go down and visit with Brentwood before dinner."

"You're not going to wait for me?" Allison whined.

"No, I'm sure you want to make an entrance and if I'm behind you it will not be as dramatic."

"Oh well, you are right there. Very well, I will be along directly." She nodded before her mask was set fully back in place and her tongue slit in two again.

When Carson arrived downstairs, Alton was standing in the hallway. He directed her to the parlor. She smiled and slipped into the room. It was beautifully and elegantly decorated. It had been updated since she had been here last. Lady Randolph was a natural at making things look more elegant than they really were.

"Carson," Jamie's deep voice came from the corner of the room. She looked up and met his gaze. "Are you alone?" He smiled devilishly and stood up from his chair.

"You look lovely this evening." She felt her cheeks grow hot as he crossed the room.

"Maybe I should go back upstairs and wait for Allison. It's not right for us to be alone."

"You are correct, but we are old friends and I do not see the danger in that." She shifted her gaze to his lips and then looked up again. Her heart began to beat wildly when he drew only a few feet away. She took in a ragged breath. "I best go back upstairs."

"Why?" The look on his face was a cross between puzzlement and teasing.

"I've already told you."

"Carson, we do not worry about things like that here in the country. We have been alone plenty of times."

"Yes, but we were children. Now we are grown and you could marry my cousin."

"I don't think that will happen."

"Why? You've only just met her."

"I didn't like the way she treated you when you first arrived." James looked somewhat embarrassed all of a sudden and gave her a sheepish smile. "I was hiding in the shadows and heard everything," James confessed. Carson's face flamed, but he pressed on. "Why do you let her treat you like that?"

"I don't know, maybe because I'm at the mercy of her family; they are the only ones who would take me in when my mother died."

"I can't believe that."

"Aunt Aggie and Uncle Charles were in France at the time. When they returned my father had already made the arrangements for me to stay with Lord Rankin. He knew I would be able to move about in society and find a husband."

"But you have not found one."

"No, I have many male acquaintances, but no husband."

"I am sure that the men of your acquaintance are blind."

"I am in Allison's shadow."

"The men are blind or see only what they want to see."

"Does that include you?" Carson winced inwardly at her thoughtless remark. He looked thoughtful for a moment and then stepped closer. Carson swallowed the lump that was forming in her throat.

"No Carson, I have always seen everything, noticed every wonderful thing about you." His voice was soft and deep.

"What wonderful things?" Her voice was breathless. He took another step closer. Her eyes drifted to his lips again and she realized he was looking at hers as well. She took a deep breath as he touched her cheek. She looked into his eyes and he closed the distance slowly. His lips lightly brushed hers and lingered.

"You're so beautiful." He breathed the words lightly against her lips and then he kissed her again.

The door clicked as if someone was opening it and both of them took several steps apart. Brentwood entered, assessed the situation, and then frowned. "It's not a good idea that you two are alone in a room behind closed doors. Allison will be furious." He had a twinkle in his eye at the last statement and Jamie laughed. "I'm not worried what Allison thinks."

Carson shifted uncomfortably trying to figure out something to say to change the conversation. "Brentwood, how are your parents?" He shot his cousin an amused look and saw her red face. "They will be arriving anytime. Lord and Lady Randolph have invited them for dinner. They are excited about seeing you, I might add. I sent word that you were with Allison." She smiled. "I may go home with them for a few days."

"They would enjoy your company," Brentwood said.

"Carson?" James said with some surprise in his voice. "Do you not want to stay here at the manor?" She shifted her gaze to Jamie.

He was so handsome and so sweet. He thinks I'm beautiful. But he is supposed to be getting to know Allison.

"I think it would be wise if I go visit my aunt and uncle. It's Allison that you should worry about."

"I told you already, I'm not going to marry Miss Rankin. She is beautiful but I see no depth there."

"You need to get to know her."

"Carson." Brentwood's voice held an air of authority and she quickly looked up. "Why are you defending her? She is always so rude to you. Why do you think I wouldn't marry her? I couldn't stand the way she treated you."

"That's why you left?" Carson said and glanced at Jamie. He looked as astonished as she.

"Allison Rankin was the one from last season?" Brentwood and Carson shifted their eyes to Jamie. "You and Allison?" James asked. He wasn't angry; on the contrary, he was smiling and then began to laugh. "Why did you not tell me when I invited you for the week?"

Brentwood only shrugged and James studied his friend for a long moment.

"You're in love with her."

"What? You're mad to think that I could love her."

"But you do." Carson's voice was soft and it caught both men's attention. "You do love her and she still loves you."

"She loves me?" Brentwood's voice was filled with astonishment.

"Yes, and if you would just admit that you are in love with her too, then you two could be together."

"I will admit it, but I cannot stand the way she treats you! She talks down to you as if you were a servant. I would not even speak to my servant like she speaks to you and you take it. Why do you take it?"

"I have no choice. My mother died and my father is on a ship, and I see him maybe once every few years."

"Come live with us at the estate. My mother and father would love for you to come live with us. I'll ask them tonight."

"Why, will that solve your problem with Allison? Do you think that she will come around if I'm not there to abuse?" Both men studied her for a moment.

"This has nothing to do with Allison and her attitude toward you. It has to do with your happiness and you can't tell me that you're happy living under Lord Rankin's roof." She looked down.

"No, I cannot, but I also cannot see how that will help you."

"To know that you're happy and safe is all I want."

"Why, Brentwood?"

"Because I love you as if you were my sister. You practically were when we were young, and I can't stand by and watch Allison treat you badly."

"You love me that much to give up loving Allison?" There was a noise in the hallway and both men turned away.

"Answer me?" Her voice was just above a whisper. He turned back to her.

"It was something else that drove me away."

"What?"

"Lord Rankin."

"What?" She gasped. "But why?"

"He wanted Allison to marry James. I didn't know who it was at the time, but now it makes perfect sense. He took a dislike to me from the start."

"I'm not going to marry her. She would never be happy with me here at the manor, and you know how I dislike town."

Brentwood smiled. "I know, why do you think I agreed to come and stay a week here? Much can change in a week."

"Many things can change in just a few hours." Carson said softly and then looked at Jamie who only smiled. Brentwood chuckled. "So the old flame you held for my fair cousin is still there?" Jamie shifted his gaze to the door.

Lord and Lady Brentwood and Lord and Lady Randolph strolled through the door while in deep conversation. The foursome only glanced up before returning to their conversation. Then Aggie realized that her niece was standing beside her son.

"Oh Carson, I was hoping you would come with Allison!" She swept across the room and embraced the young woman who looked so much like herself that she could have easily been mistaken for her daughter.

"Yes, I insisted that I come. I was planning on visiting you while Allison and Mr. Randolph get to know each other."

James stepped forward and put his hand on her elbow. "But she has changed her mind. We are running off to Gretna Green tonight." Both ladies gasped and the men began to laugh. "He is joking about Gretna Green. I would never do anything so foolish," Carson said.

"It's scandalous just to talk that way James. And besides you've Miss Rankin to entertain."

"Not really, that is what Brentwood is here for."

"Oh no . . . you leave me out of that conversation!" Everyone laughed. Carson walked over to where her cousin was standing and looped her arm through his. "You and Allison could run off to Gretna Green, and no one would even know until she sent word to her parents to send her things to your estate."

"Carson!" Aggie gasped. "As much as I would love to see my son happily married, we will not discuss him running off to Gretna Green, or you, for that matter."

"I agree." Catherine Randolph said as she reached Carson and pulled her into a hug. "It is so good to see you, Carson. You look so much like Aggie these days. You are so beautiful with all those auburn curls."

"Thank you." She accepted the woman's hug and cherished the love she felt from these two women. She missed her mother so much at times, but these women were like her mother in so many ways.

Suddenly Allison swept into the room with her beautiful gown and her hair up in a beautiful fashion. Her dress was similar to Carson's except it was pale green. She crossed the room with a brilliant smile. "Good evening."

"Good evening, Miss Rankin." Lord Randolph said as he took her hand and bowed over it. She smiled up at the older Randolph and then to Lord Brentwood who did the same. The older women greeted her and went back to their conversation with Carson.

Carson gave Allison a warm smile and she hesitantly joined the women. Jamie and Brentwood walked over to the fireplace. Jamie studied his best friend as he watched Allison. "I have to admit that she is beautiful, but she is not for me. I have loved Carson for so long that I can't imagine marrying anyone else."

"You sound so sure of that."

"I have to say it has been a long time and she has changed from that girl I used to kiss in the maze, but when I looked into her green eyes, I knew that she was someone I could love forever."

"Carson will make you a wonderful wife. I can't imagine her with anyone else. Though she had many men seeking her hand at balls and parties, very few ever dared to approach the Rankin house. Lord Rankin is somewhat of a bear. He basically told me not to come back to court his daughter. That she was to marry someone else."

"Who?"

"You."

James laughed. "I know that is what our families want but surely they are not expecting it. We don't know each other. She is not someone who is in the same circle as the Randolph family, and we rarely go to town."

"Are you saying that you're better than her?"

"No, of course not, she is a gentleman's daughter. What I am saying is, I do not like moving in society and she is a social butterfly. Allison would never be happy here in the country."

"Do you think that Carson would be content here at Randolph Manor?"

"Not completely, but if she loves me and I love her, then we will make compromises for each other."

"And you think Allison will not compromise?"

"No, I do not." Jamie shook his head.

"I see, so are you telling me I'm free to pursue Allison?"

Jamie smiled. "Are you saying that I have your blessing to marry Carson?"

"You don't need my blessing, but I would count it an honor to be related to you."

"Then you better go and woo Miss Rankin. For she is only here for a week and if her father refused you before, he may do it again unless she stands up for you."

Brentwood nodded. "Indeed."

Alton came and announced that dinner was being served. The older couples filed out and Jamie smiled at the two ladies left in the room as he and Brentwood approached. "Miss Rankin, Brentwood and I have been talking. We believe that it is wise that he escort you to dinner." Allison looked up at Brentwood and then back to James. "May I ask why?"

James looked at Carson and replied, "Because I know that I do not want to marry you. I'm in love with someone else. And let's face it. You would not be happy with me." Allison looked at Carson and then to Brentwood.

"What did you tell him about me?"

"I didn't have to tell him anything," Brentwood said casually. "He is in love with Carson and has been for years. Besides I'm in love with you and if it weren't for your father you would already be my wife. Now take my arm Allison and let me escort you to dinner." She gasped but didn't reply and then took his arm. She refused to look at him and her spin was stiff as they walked out.

Carson took Jamie's arm and they left the room, but Brentwood hung back for a moment and turned to Alison.

"If you say one cruel word to Carson this week, I will never have you as a wife."

His eyes were steel gray and she knew that he was serious. "I will do as you ask." She gave him a genuine smile that lit up her eyes. "Do you really love me?"

He smiled down at her. "With all my heart."

"I love you too, Brentwood. Oh how I love you, too." He lowered his head and kissed her sweetly then pulled away. "We need to get to dinner." She nodded and he led her away.

Carson and James were standing in the hallway kissing as the other couple reached it. James stepped back stiffly when Brentwood cleared his throat. "She isn't your wife yet, James." James only shrugged. "I have been stealing kisses from her for years. Why stop now that I plan to marry her?"

Brentwood chuckled. Carson blushed and looked at Allison.

Carson realized that this was the exact spot where they stood that afternoon when both she and Allison were miserable, but now they were both with the men they truly loved. It was amazing how entering the door to Randolph Manor could change their lives forever!

Sitting on Plastic

Doris Gwaltney

There was an itch at the old man's scalp. Every time he came down to the hospital restaurant, it started. He knew what caused it, too. It was the padded back of the dining booth, and the edge of the table. His shoulders wavered back and forth. He didn't want to touch either of them. They were smelly. Dirty.

Oh God, his head itched. He knew what his wife Lessie would say if she were here. She didn't like him to scratch his head in public. But she wasn't here. It was his daughter Gloria who was sitting across from him, chewing on a sandwich as big as a small loaf of bread. The girl was fat. Getting fatter every day.

The itch got the better of him and he started to scratch. He rubbed on and on, sifting now and then a single scale of dandruff onto his dark suit.

"Look here," his daughter was saying. "You can't keep a red stool on a red carpet. It's no wonder she fell. I fell once, too. Course I didn't break anything."

"A bit too much padding for that," the old man said.

"What did you say?"

"I don't remember saying anything."

Gloria took another bite of her sandwich. Her mouth twisted and bounced. Then her lips bulged forward as she shifted the shredded cheese, and turkey, and lettuce, and bread.

The old man looked away. He didn't want to hear another word about it. They had a right to put their red leather hassock wherever they chose.

"I've told Mother and I've told her. She's eighty-five years old and it's time she realized it. Older people cannot go on as they've always done."

He'd heard enough about older people and what they could and couldn't do. He was a few years older than Lessie. He was ninety, to be exact. But he didn't feel old. His mind wasn't old. His left leg was a bit stiff, but his right leg was the one that did all the work anyway. His vision was good, except that he did wear reading glasses he bought at the drugstore. He didn't need to wear a hearing aid. Sometimes he wished he did. One he could turn off when his daughter was on one of her tirades. She talked with her mouth full. He never had been able to teach her anything. No manners. Not a bone in her body was like Lessie.

"And look at you, Dad," she was saying. "Here you are, ninety years old, and won't walk with a cane. Won't wear a hearing aid."

"Gloria, I can hear."

"Now, I don't believe that. You don't answer my questions. You don't laugh at jokes. Which plainly says to me you're deaf as a post."

"I can hear, Gloria."

"Dad, you can't. But that's not the problem we're facing here today. Read my lips. Whatever. But you've got to listen to me because something has to be done now."

"Why now? Why can't things go on as they are?"

Gloria took a deep breath, then slowly let it out between clenched lips.

"They can't go on because you'll starve to death. You haven't had a decent meal since Mother got hurt. Now eat your salad."

"I hate salads."

He looked across the room at the steam table, the fat women ladling out heaping plates and bowls and cups and saucers. An avalanche of food and not one bite of it fit to eat. He hated all of it. He hated the slippery red plastic he was sitting on. Hated his cut up salad, sitting like garbage on a black plastic bowl.

"You have to eat something, Dad."

Lessie had been a renowned cook in her day. Back when they were young, he would come into the kitchen to find her leaning across the table, making bread. She placed the palms of her hands on the dough and pushed down with her arms. She threw her whole body into it. Almost left the floor when she got going.

She was a little woman, with narrow hips, a thin waist, and remarkable posture. He had never seen her slump in her entire life. She still didn't. Lying upstairs in that hospital bed, she was straight as an arrow. Weighed nothing like a hundred pounds and never had. Except when she was carrying Gloria.

Now that was another story. They'd waited years for Lessie to get pregnant. And it happened only the once.

"Dad, as soon as you're finished . . ."

Women nowadays weren't like Lessie. At least Gloria surely wasn't. When she graduated from college, he tried to talk her into being a teacher like he and her mother. But, no. Nothing would do but to get married. He and Lessie accepted that and life went on. For a few years.

But then she got restless. She complained about everything. So then he tried to talk to her about being a better wife and mother. Right off the bat she asked him if a woman had the talent to paint a picture or write a book, shouldn't she do it? He answered yes, of course, and thought that was an end of it. He prepared himself to compliment her little drawings and stories. But she took a test and went to selling real estate. Poking around in other people's houses, kicking furnaces, and scratching at the paint.

"I won't sell a bad house," she'd said. "You don't get ahead palming off rat traps. I plan to be known as an honest agent."

Her husband, who started divorce proceedings three weeks after she went to work, questioned her honesty in several other matters. Matters with several men. He was fairly sure Lessie knew nothing, but he himself knew about three men. One was a plumber who came to check out a bathroom commode. One was the children's pediatrician. And one sold books door to door. Likely she got her ideas about a woman's talent from him.

Anyway, she got the divorce, and the husband let her have custody of the children. He thought he understood that, too. Who would want them? Two hulking boys, as puffed up fat as Gloria. They were the ones who needed canes. Applied, not in walking.

Still, they did do their own cooking. He would hand them that. Gloria did no more for them than to load up bags of frozen food at the grocery store, bring it home, and stick it in the freezer. They chewed and swallowed at all hours. Every day of the week.

"Dad, are you listening to me?"

"Yes . . . well, to be honest, no. What did you say?"

"I said you have to eat. We need to get back to Mother."

"I have no appetite."

"Jesus Christ."

"Your mother wouldn't like that, Gloria."

"Oh, come off it, Dad."

Gloria shook her head and rolled her eyes at some person behind him, out of his line of vision.

"Look now," she went on. "I have this appointment to show a house across town at three o'clock. I don't have much time, and I mean to get something settled today. So you might as well face up to it. Mother's going to be an invalid. The doctor said so."

"Gloria, no . . . Your mother may be frail, but she's strong."

"Dad, I know what the doctor says. Mother won't be able to do the housework, or cook, or shop for groceries. And you sure don't know how. And I'm too busy a person to look after two houses. Now I've been wanting to build a couple of rooms onto my house for some time. Maybe you heard me say so."

He had indeed heard her say so. For the past five years she'd been saying so. First she called it a rumpus room, and he agreed with her that if anyone in the world knew how to make use of a rumpus room, it was she. Lately she'd called it a Florida room. She described it as something like an animal cage, as he saw it. Sliding glass doors. Made you feel like you were outdoors. Now if he wanted to feel like he was outdoors, he would open the door and go out. And when he was inside his house, he wanted privacy. He would fight for his privacy.

"So I've decided, Dad. . . ."

"You've decided?"

"Somebody had to. And it's high time to sell your house. I've got a builder who can do a rush job. Two rooms on my house. That's all we need."

And when we're dead and gone, he thought to himself, you can make a rumpus in your Florida room.

Gloria had gone out the front door of the hospital to smoke. He had given up smoking the very hour he first saw a cigarette in his daughter's mouth. She looked so silly. He wondered if he looked silly, too, holding a little white cylinder in his mouth. So that was the end of it. It was probably the reason he was so healthy at age ninety.

He walked around the lobby, all four sides, until he saw Gloria walking through the entry doors.

"Let's sit down for a while. We need to talk and I don't want to upset Mother."

This time he leaned back into the plastic curve of the chair. He was tired. He closed his eyes.

"Wake up, Dad."

He opened his own eyes and looked into her blue ones, the same color as Lessie's. She had one of those kinky permanents where you wash your hair, shake it once or twice, and go right on. "It always looks the same," she'd told them. He nodded his head back to her in agreement. It did always look the same. Terrible.

"Now this is it, Dad. This is the way I see it. I've tried hinting. I've tried coaxing. I've told you how good it would be for you to spend more time with your grandchildren."

Oh, yes, he thought. Splendid.

"And I would be able to cook for you and Mother."

He could picture Gloria jangling her bracelets into the freezer, then later, pushing the buttons on the microwave.

"I could see that the house is clean and the laundry done. Or, I don't know, Dad, you need something to do. Maybe you can do the cleaning."

He could see himself dusting the Florida room. An aviary. Probably dead leaves would blow in. Moss would grow.

"So what I mean is, I'm putting my foot down. I'm listing your house this very afternoon. It ought to go fast. Lots of people these days are into Victorian. They like fixer-uppers. Like to paint them bright colors, and rip out partitions, and use flood lights on the stained glass."

"Gloria, look here.

He had never been able to talk to Gloria properly. He usually sent her messages through Lessie. "Lessie, talk to Gloria," he would say.

Lessie had been the one to walk to the door of the darkened parlor and call out: "Bedtime," when it seemed to all intents and purposes that Gloria and her young man had already made the transition. It was Lessie who told her they couldn't set up that poor husband of hers in a dry cleaning business. That they wouldn't keep the grandchildren and the cat every weekend. Wouldn't pay for her damned rumpus room.

He wanted Lessie now. He needed her to tell this girl they had never, in sixty years of marriage needed anybody's help. Lessie would heal. And he could learn to help around the house.

"Look here," he said again. "I won't leave my own home."

"Okay, I might as well level with you. Mother gave me power of attorney a couple of months ago. I've already listed the house. In fact, it's the one I'm showing at 3:00. I've got a hot buyer. Wants immediate occupancy. Won't notice a thing. He just wants to get those kids out of a motel room."

He was dizzy. To think of it . . . Lessie had given Gloria power of attorney. But without his knowledge, was that legal? He'd call his lawyer the minute he got home. But then he heard a strange voice calling out to them on the intercom.

"Will Gloria McCartney and Mr. Talbot report to the third floor?"
"Come on, Dad, let's go."

When they reached the third floor, Gloria ran off ahead of him. He was breathing heavily, and he felt like his legs weren't actually moving. They were so heavy. He stepped and stepped. By the time he reached the double swinging doors, she was already through and halfway down the hall. He followed slowly, very slowly behind her.

Gloria was standing beside a large chrome cart, with tubes, and nozzles and plastic see-through bags of clear liquid. What was it?

He could hear the distant tinkle of Gloria's bracelets, and he could feel the sound of it all over his body. He leaned against the wall and watched the commotion, watched Gloria take the nurse by the arm and stare into her face. The chrome and black machine on wheels was standing stationary now in front of one of the bedrooms. He leaned sideways to read the numbers. 318. Lessie's room.

Why were nurses and a machine standing idle at the door of Lessie's room? He forced himself to walk, his right shoulder digging hard against the wall.

"Oh God," he heard Gloria say. "I don't know what I'll ever do with him." And then she began to cry.

"Gloria, what is it?" he said. "What's the matter with you? Lessie, you'll have to talk to the child. Tell her not to cry. Tell her she can't sell the house. Tell her, Lessie."

The door of Lessie's room opened and a man in a green coat came out. A doctor. He shook Gloria's hand, and said he was sorry. "Blood clot . . . sudden . . . right to the heart . . ."

Was this man saying that Lessie was . . . dead? That she could never tell Gloria not to sell the house? Not to feed him garbage on a black plastic plate? He stared at the green and tan painted wall. He pressed his fingers tight against it, for his legs that had seemed so heavy a few moments before, had turned weightless. His feet kept wanting to lift, his legs to follow. His whole body was bent on levitation. He pushed harder with the pads of his fingers, but the walls began to dissolve. He was alone, illuminated by blinding sunlight. It crashed all around him through glass walls.

He bowed his head as his fingers came unstuck from the walls. His shoulders grew limp. He began to weave and sway. His daughter led him back down the hallway and seated him in a red plastic chair.

The Pony That Looked West

Elaine Habermehl

My new car came to a grinding stop in the middle of a Washington, DC, street. This is not supposed to happen to new cars, but it is how I met the woman sitting on the bench at the bus stop directly opposite my stalled car.

Aggie Brown was a rather large woman. The end of her rested on the middle of a wooden bench. As I walked away from the tow truck, she slid down the bench making room for me.

As an eyewitness to the traffic tie up around my stalled car, she said she hoped I had good shoes; shoes that would carry me far, seeing that I would be walking the long blocks between bus stops soon. In fifteen minutes, a cross-town bus would deliver me to a neighborhood far away from Aggies's world. A place of green lawns, warm brick houses, and neighbors I did not know. A place as unfamiliar to Aggie as her world was to me.

She gave a disapproving frown when she looked down at my shiny black high heels. A white umbrella covered her own feet. She used the umbrella as a shield against the brown icy slush that tires churned onto the sidewalk while turning the corner.

When the traffic quieted, she moved the umbrella enough to show me her dark leather western boots, just as shiny as new, but worn down at the heel. I could see she had taken great care of them. She leaned against me, "It's important to have good shoes, and of course polish is key."

Under a massive gray coat, she wore a white apron knotted at the back of her neck. The apron hung below the hem of her coat and brushed the tops of the newspaper-stuffed boots. The green coffee can at her feet filled daily with money. When the offerings were large, she would quickly pick up the can ready to make change, but her supporters refused and walked on. She had an accent, but not from this corner of the world. When I asked her where she was from, she became quiet and wistful. She sang a line from a song I used to know, "where the deer and the antelope play." "West," she said.

On day five of my bus-riding adventure, she pulled a folded leather pouch from a pocket inside her coat. Untying the string, she placed the pouch on my lap. The tools inside were worn but shiny. Slim fingers pointed to each tool as she explained their use. There was a hoof knife and nippers, a rasp for the teeth of a horse, shoe nails, brushes and curry combs, but most vital of all, a hoof gaffer for correcting the balance of horseshoes. "It's important to have good shoes, even if you have four feet," she said. A little silver horse dangled from a length of white dental floss inside the pouch.

Aggie Brown polished the stone ponies of Washington, DC. Some had riders, some did not. She explained that there were twenty-eight ponies in Washington and that all faced the White House save one, her favorite she said. He looked west.

In time, my car was repaired and returned. My most enjoyable time with Aggie Brown came to an end. I turned the corner of Aggie's street nearly every day on my way to work. The pointed toes of her boots peaked from under the white umbrella balanced on her legs. In time, the cold slush disappeared and Aggies's bus stop dried as the earth around it sprouted new green grass. I made a point of visiting every equestrian statue in Washington. Every so often, I would glimpse Aggie in her white apron, carefully brushing a stone pony as lovingly as the ones she'd tended in a another place far from here.

The pony that faced west was especially well-cared for; his stone body stood gleaming in the spring sun. He wore no bridle or saddle and held one foot in the air as if ready to take a step with his rider, a woman with soft brown eyes that looked west.

Watch Birds

Elaine Habermehl

Claire awoke with a start and turned over to glance at the luminous dial of her alarm clock. Four ten in the morning, and the dog down the street was barking. Soon the black car would roar past her house and turn onto the main highway. She padded across the bedroom floor to the open window and stood in the curtains' shadow, waiting. Claire watched the house on the corner, its front entrance bathed in moonlight.

The car window rolled down slowly, a hand emerged, twisted the mailbox latch letting the door drop open. She watched as the envelope was deposited, and the mailbox closed. It was all over in an instant.

The car pulled away from the driveway, its driver a blur as the car drove away. Who was it she wondered? Curiosity was getting the best of her. She was spending more and more time behind her bedroom curtain and less time sleeping.

Claire wished it wasn't so early, she was frightened and needed to talk. She tied the bathrobe securely around her waist and walked downstairs to the kitchen. Dunking a tea bag into her cup, she waited for the water to boil. She cradled the cup in her hands and slid into a chair to wait for dawn.

Agnes looked down at her wristwatch as the phone rang. Seven in the morning was a little early for a phone call. She popped the last bite of muffin into her mouth and walked down the hall to the phone. "Hello."

"Hi, Agnes, it's Claire."

"Are you O.K?"

"I'm fine, but I've got so much to tell you I couldn't wait any longer."

"What's going on?" Agnes asked anxiously.

"That black car was in the neighborhood again last night. There was another envelope delivered to the Bernardo's mailbox," she said all in one breath.

Agnes sighed. Claire was certainly living up to her role in the neighborhood as nosy neighbor.

"Why are you up at such an early hour spying on the neighbors?"

"I'm not spying," Claire huffed. "Anyway, their dog woke me, so I got up to look out the window."

"I'm almost afraid to ask, but what do you think is in the envelopes?" Agnes questioned.

"Messages, and meeting times," she whispered. "I'll bet he's a spy!"

"And, how can you be so sure?" Agnes said sarcastically.

"Because I opened one last week," Claire countered.

There was a sharp intake of breath from Agnes. "What, you opened his mail?"

"It wasn't really mail. There was no stamp, no address, just an envelope with his name typed on the front."

"It's still mail, Claire; even you can't rationalize this." Agnes's patience was reaching its outer limits fast. Claire had done some silly things, but this was too much.

"I sealed it up with a little glue and put it back. He'll never know."

Agnes drew a breath then coughed into the mouthpiece, excused herself and ran to get a glass of water. She raked a hand through her fine gray hair. "Well, now that you've got my curiosity up, are you going to tell me what it said?"

"First of all it was typed in capital letters, there was no signature so I don't know who it was from," she said excitedly.

Agnes forced herself to keep a level voice. "You're stalling, what did it say?" Claire whispered into the phone, "J. Bernardo, contact us at noon tomorrow."

Agnes felt a prickly sensation creep along her spine. "What, are you sure?"

"Of course I'm sure, I know what I saw! Now at exactly 4:10 every morning, a car stops at the Bernardo's mailbox and leaves an envelope."

"I think you should leave the Bernardo's and their mailbox alone, that's what I think!" Agnes stressed.

"'I think I should call the police," Claire whispered into the mouthpiece. "But first I'd like another look inside one of those envelopes before I call anyone."

"And how are you going to do that?" Agnes wondered.

"I'll simply be nearby when the next one is delivered, read it, then put it back; he'll never know," Claire said in her most self-assured voice.

"What if the police come by? What if your picture makes the front of the *Post* tomorrow morning? Have you thought about what could happen?" Agnes questioned.

"None of that's going to happen, because you'll be with me; I'm going to need an extra pair of eyes tonight. I don't want to be out at that hour by myself, Agnes. Can you please go with me?"

Irritated with her friend, "Claire, I'm not going, this is crazy." Agnes didn't want to go, but also didn't want Claire to be alone. She knew Claire would do this deed by herself if needed. Thirty years of friendship had proven that.

"Do you remember the time you forgot to pick me up at the train station? It was snowing, as I remember. I was wet by the time the cab came. Then there is the matter of the cold I caught. Do you remember? I mean really," Claire hissed.

"Oh no, here we go down memory lane. I would have picked you up, Claire, if you would have only given me the right date."

"Remember when you broke your wrist and I cleaned your cat's litter box for a full month? You owe me for that one, Agnes. Where is that cat anyway?"

"I believe I said thank you, and Poppy is keeping my feet warm at the moment."

"Nevertheless. What about the time you burned a cigarette hole in the leather upholstery of my brand new car and put a bunion patch over it thinking I wouldn't see? What do you say to that, Agnes?"

"I am truly sorry about that. But that bunion patch held a remarkable likeness to the leather even if I do say so myself." Agnes bit her tongue remembering the bunion patch incident, trying not to laugh.

"We need to do this, Agnes; it is our civic duty! Maybe the safety of the neighborhood is in jeopardy."

"We?" Agnes questioned.

"Yes, we, please?"

"Oh, all right." Agnes, now exhausted from the verbal battle, accepted her fate. Claire was once again cheerful.

"Great! Wear something dark; I think there's a full moon tonight."

Agnes slipped a small flashlight into her jacket pocket before she went outside. Summertime in Washington was usually hot and humid, but not tonight. The stars were out, and a breeze had the tops of tall trees swaying.

Claire jumped, putting a hand over her fluttering heart as Agnes walked up behind her.

"This is stupid, Claire; I don't know how I let you talk me into this."

"Shh! Do you want to wake the neighborhood? You should have covered that gray hair of yours, it's going to stand out like a beacon in the moonlight."

"Sorry, I haven't quite gotten the spy game down yet," Agnes said haughtily.

"Come on. Let's go, it's almost time," Claire whispered. The two women moved away from Claire's back door.

Avoiding the streetlights as much as possible, they walked softly down the sidewalk. Claire led the way to the Bernardo's yard. Picking their way across cold dew covered grass, they paused under the limbs of a pine tree at the corner of the yard. Leaning against the stone fence that surrounded the house, they waited.

Agnes tapped the glowing dial of her wristwatch. Claire turned to look: 4:09. The car should be here soon. Sure enough, there was a whine of a car engine in the distance. Looking around the corner of the house, they watched the dark sedan pull up to the driveway.

As a hand appeared from the car window and unlatched the mailbox, they held their breath. The hand that clicked the mailbox closed woke the dog in the backyard and instantly it started barking. The hand disappeared inside the car as the window rolled closed. The car hastened away.

Claire waited for the dog to go back to sleep before she made a move toward the mailbox. Agnes watched and waited, hoping this would all be over soon and they could go home. Claire was back in seconds holding a white envelope. Agnes produced the flashlight from her pocket. The glue on the envelope was still moist and the flap lifted easily.

Agnes trained the flashlight on the letter as Claire pulled it from the envelope and turned it over to read. Their eyes grew wide as they looked down at the paper. "J. Bernardo, contact us at one o'clock tomorrow," it read.

Claire's hands trembled as she pushed the message back into the envelope. She pressed the flap down with her fingertips hoping it would seal. Holding it in her outstretched palm she waited for the flap to come loose. When it did, she turned to Agnes. "Agnes, hand me the glue." Claire waved the open envelope under Agnes's nose.

"What glue? You didn't ask me to bring any glue," Agnes said through clenched teeth.

"I did! What are we going to do? We can't put it back like this!" Claire was losing her nerve rapidly.

"We're going to need more than glue. The lights in the Bernardo's house just came on! Put it back! That car didn't make the turn at the corner. It's just sitting there." Panic had become Agnes's cloak.

Arm and arm they crept back down the wet grass to the mailbox. They opened and closed the little door silently, careful to hold the flag so it didn't jiggle and wake the dog.

Then they were off, back to Claire's house as fast as their legs would carry them. Inside, Agnes put water in the kettle to boil. Claire turned the pages of the phone book on her lap.

"I think we should skip calling the police. Call the FBI instead," Agnes said nervously. "Something's wrong. You said the lights are never on in the Bernardo's house after the envelope's dropped."

"That's right, never. Here's the number for the FBI. I think the driver saw us. I saw a flash of light from the car. Do you think he took a picture of us?" Claire asked.

Later on, Agnes was pouring boiling water over the tea leaves in Claire's cup when the doorbell rang. Claire glanced at her watch; it was 8:30 a.m. Hot water splashed into the saucer of the tea cup. The two women exchanged looks of alarm, stopping all movement, afraid even to breathe. The doorbell rang out again, echoing down the hall and into Claire's cozy kitchen.

Claire led the way down the narrow hallway to the door with Agnes following close behind.

The two women peered through the glass pane near the door to find a rather large official-looking man standing on the doorstep. He wore a hat and carried a large manila envelope under one arm.

"Should we open the door?" Claire whispered.

Agnes shrugged, her eyes fearful. Claire took a long breath, her hand resting on the lock, then turned the doorknob.

"I'm sorry to call on you at such an early hour. I'm Sean Whelen." He reached into the inside pocket of his jacket. The women took a step back from the door. "Agent Sean Whelen." The man grinned as he opened the leather cover on his badge and picture. "Can I come in?"

The women moved aside, letting Agent Whelen close the door behind him. He turned to the two nervous women standing before him.

"Are you Miss Claire Higgins?"
"Yes."
"And you are?" he said, looking at Agnes.
"Miss Agnes, Agnes Northern."
"Our agency is in the process of gathering information on your neighbor, Mr. J. Bernardo. Do you know him?"

Claire gave her friend a sideways look, her eyebrows raised.

"I've never spoken to him, but I've seen him on occasion," Claire answered.

"Any strange behavior? You know, something you've noticed maybe, just passing a window?"

Claire led the way to the kitchen where she nervously wiped up the pools of spilled tea.

Agent Whelen opened the manila envelope and spread black and white photos across the kitchen table. There were pictures of their neighbor in question picking up mail from various mailboxes around the city, standing on the arch of a bridge talking with another man, eating with a couple at a restaurant, walking alone across a well-known street downtown.

"I don't understand," Claire whispered across the table.

"We believe J. Bernardo is here on a covert mission Miss Higgins."

Claire shot Agnes a knowing look.

"Sometimes answers can be discovered by chance, just on close observation." Agent Whelen moved all but the last three pictures in the pile aside. He pushed these across the table so Claire and Agnes could have a closer look. They looked down at their own black and white images. One picture at the neighbor's mailbox, another leaning against the Bernardo's stone fence. The last picture of two dimly lit female faces pondering a white envelope under a flashlight beam. Agnes rubbed her now tired eyes, trying to erase the images before her. She turned and mouthed the words "told you," to Claire.

"Any information you have could be of help, Miss Higgins." Agent Whelen retuned the stack of pictures to the manila envelope, then leaned back in his chair, waiting.

"Well, Agent Whelen, I'm a light sleeper and I glanced out the window . . .

Rainy Night in Wilhering

Keppel Hagerman

Rain pelted so hard against the windows of our rented VW, we could barely make out the outline of the Gasthaus Wilhering. George shouted over the din, "Ruth, go see if we can get a room. I'll keep the motor running."

I ran up the steps and rang the bell by the heavy oak door, which was instantly opened by a tall, slim young woman with cropped gold-brown hair and hazel eyes. I prayed that she had a room available and that she'd understand my schoolbook German. I started to sputter my request when she interrupted in crisp, lightly accented English, "Please don't worry, I speak English. Are you American?"

I gushed that yes, I was, and that my husband and I required a double room with bath for one evening.

"The place is yours. We have no other guest; the summer season is past, and in this weather tourists will not be coming to the gardens of Wilhering's famous Cistercian Abbey."

I didn't tell her that our reason for being in this isolated spot was not the Abbey but our curiosity to see the town where Adolph Hitler was born, supposedly another 25 kilometers down the road.

The woman handed me a large key on a red tag. Before I ran out to George, I asked, "Are you English?"

"No," she replied. "I'm from a small village near Johannesburg in South Africa. We serve dinner at seven o'clock. My husband Emil is an excellent chef."

I waved to her, ran out the door to find George staring from the car window. He started pulling the bags from the car.

No let up in the rain, but he laughed as we climbed the steps, always cheered at the end of a day's travel with the prospect of a drink, hot dinner, and sleep.

The open door revealed two narrow beds covered with prim

white spreads, two very straight chairs, a night table and an oak bureau.

"Wow, what a cozy little spot," muttered George.

"It's cold, too," I said. Already dusk was settling in.

The black iron table lamp produced the equivalent of a 20-watter. We could see nothing outside through the teeming rain.

For a while, we sat in silence, sipping the last of the bourbon we had brought from Virginia.

"Maybe it wasn't such a good idea to detour through Wilhering so we could find Hitler's home town," said George. "This isn't exactly the charm we found in the Austrian Tyrol."

"Well, at least we'll be able to get a good night's sleep. It's almost seven, let's go down to dinner."

We descended the narrow steps and passed through a small cheerless sitting room in which a fire was laid, but unlit.

From the windows, we could see the heavy gray rain. Across the road loomed the bulk of large buildings, the Abbey, we presumed. In the adjoining dining room we were accosted by the throaty sound of German being spoken loudly and rapidly. The dining room cheered us with its saucy red curtains and sparkling white napkins which adorned each table. Two men in work clothes sat at one of the tables, a third in a white shirt and black bow tie stood by them. They were in deep conversation. The tall blond one in the white shirt came over to us. In heavily accented English he said, "You are the Americans, yes? My wife has told me. I am Chef Emil. I welcome you to my guest house."

He gave a little bow, but no smile lightened his face. Then he led us to a table brightened surprisingly by a bouquet of lavender chrysanthemums.

"You will sit, please, and I will bring dinner."

I tried to smile, as I asked, "And where is your wife this evening?"

"Ah, Janetta, she will come later." With another tight bow he vanished into what had to be the kitchen.

"He's not a bunch of laughs, is he?" George nodded toward the kitchen.

"And his wife was so pleasant," I said. "I hope he's as good a cook as she promised."

The two men left the room without glancing our way. In a few minutes, Emil placed steaming bowls of soup in front of us. "An Austrian dish," he announced, "Leberknodelsuppe." It was delicious; we began to revive.

Herr Chef then presented a full bottle of wine in a green bottle and poured us each a glass. When he returned, he brought two plates of roast pork, red cabbage, and tiny boiled potatoes. "Guten Appetit," he pronounced, and was off again.

George and I ate greedily and fast. "Delicious," I said again, "and give me some more wine." We finished the bottle and waited. Again Emil appeared.

"You liked it, ja?"

"Ja, we liked it."

"Now I can give you plum torte mit Schlag, if you wish. In Austria we eat pastry with coffee in afternoon, but I think Americans eat it after all meals." We decided not to take this as an implied slur on our national character, but happily accepted the torte. Again, it was excellent. Finally, when there was no more to eat, the door opened and Janetta came to us. I introduced Janetta to George, and we told her how much we'd enjoyed the dinner.

"Yes, Emil is a good chef; he learned in my country."

It was then I noticed a small bird with blue, gold, and scarlet markings, perched on her shoulder.

"What a beautiful bird," I said and Janetta replied, "He's of the parrot family and comes from my region of South Africa. I call him Petit Ami, a small friend from home. When I'm homesick, I talk to him for hours."

"Are you often homesick, Janetta?" I found myself unexpectedly asking her. There was an unnatural glistening in her hazel eyes.

"South Africa is far from Austria, Madam. When I told Emil I would marry him, it was with the understanding I could return home once a year. I did for the first two years, but in the last two we could not spend the money, and Emil will not permit me to go without him."

I bet he won't. I thought to myself. He knows you might not want to leave that land of sunshine and birds and return to this dark town.

"Last year, my mother sent me Petit Ami in a cage all the way by airplane from South Africa." Then she added, "But birds of this sort, when kept caged, begin to slowly die."

There was along pause before I asked her, "How did you and Emil meet?"

"Emil came to culinary school in Johannesburg. It is a very good school, and he had an uncle who had studied there some years before. The uncle died fighting for Hitler. But now, please, tell me about your country."

George and I babbled away cheerfully, extolling the delights and virtues of the U.S.A.

Rainy Night in Wilhering

The bird clung to Janetta's shoulder. Occasionally she murmured endearments to him. She showed us how he would take a morsel of food from her mouth with his beak.

"At night he sleeps in a box near my bed. Emil is not fond of him."

As if she had called him, Herr Emil emerged from the shadows.

"Janetta, I think it is time you let our guests rest." And then he added something in rapid German I couldn't catch. Immediately Janetta stood up, took my hand and said, "I will see you at breakfast, I hope. Sleep well." She slid away, the bird clinging to her, but not before I saw her give her husband a look I tried to interpret.

As we got up to leave, Emil clapped George on the back and said he would be honored if we would look at his wine collection. It was the last thing we felt like doing, but dutifully we followed him into the next room. Here were rows of bottles in neat piles nestled deep into a bricked-in-cave arrangement. He showed us his temperature control, his eyes sparkling. It was the first warmth or enthusiasm we'd seen him display. He attempted to explain years and vintages, but it was too much for his English. Suddenly, his tone changed. In a clipped voice he said, "But the production of wine is not known to Americans."

George started to say something about California and New York State wines, but Emil was not listening.

His pale blue eyes had turned a steely gray. "It is why I do not want me or my wife to come to your country. No old history like us in Europe, no old Kultur. All new."

I could see George beginning to turn purple. He grabbed my hand and muttered under his breath, "Come on, Ruth, let's get out of here." I shouted over my shoulder, "Good night."

All the way up the steps George cursed, "Damned Nazi son of a bitch."

We clung to each other in a single bed through the dark rainy night.

By morning, the rain had stopped, but the sky was a sullen pewter. Without conversation, we threw our things in the bags. At the foot of the steps, George said, "I'll leave some money and we'll get breakfast on the road."

But at that moment Janetta appeared to lead us to the dining room. She chatted all through coffee and rolls. I was surprised to see Petit Ami across the room, sitting on a perch in a cage. When we rose to go, she clutched my hand and pressed a card in it. On it was written her name and address. "Please send me a card from the United States," she said.

I promised I would, and wrote our address for her. Then she handed us a tightly wrapped package.

"My husband asked me to give this, a bottle of his wine."

She added, "Did you know his father was party leader in this village?" She lowered her voice, "I think Emil wants to be a kind man."

My words tumbled out, "Don't keep Petit Ami in his cage too much, Janetta. Let him fly free."

Then I hugged her, and tried to ignore the tears in her eyes. "Auf Wiedersehen, Janetta!"

We were silent for the next twenty kilometers, and already on the Autobahn, when George remarked, "We never did get directions to Hitler's birthplace."

I nodded, but my thoughts were elsewhere. I knew what I'd always remember about Wilhering was a small bird languishing in a cage.

The Husky Young Man and the Nun

Robert L. Kelly

The first day's session is over. I am released from that dark hotel ballroom where we spent the whole day hassling over standardization of ammunition hoists. Now I am released to explore my wildest fantasy: New Orleans.

I had seen Ingrid Bergman's triumphant return to New Orleans from Paris in the movie *Saratoga Trunk*. I marveled at her visit to the raucous French Market to taste that most divine of all American dishes: hash. With the clamor of so many vendors demanding her attention, I wondered how she could make any choices. But she finds her hash and eats it from a plate set on her dwarf servant's top hat. Hollywood's portrayal of New Orleans in the mid-1800s showed a fantasyland that I never expected to see, but here I am just a toss away from the French Quarter. As we drove in from the airport this morning, I glimpsed houses with lacey wrought iron balconies fronting them just like in the movie. They are only a few blocks from the hotel.

I cross Canal Street, walk down its other side, pass North Rampart Street, Burgundy, Dauphine, and turn into the French Quarter on Bourbon Street. There ahead are the houses with the wrought iron balconies. I am walking right into the movie! Walking quickly down a surprisingly crude Bourbon Street, I rush across Jackson Square and head for the French Market on the levee. Still going fast, I make it to its end, turn around, change my pace to a saunter, and take in the Market sights.

I finally end up on a bench in Jackson Square. My eyes caress St. Louis Cathedral, play over the perfect symmetry of its steeples, and dwell on the ornate buildings flanking the Cathedral that give it a sense of balance and antiquity. Scanning the square, I see artists working at their easels, some with people gathered around them, watching. But for the most part the Square is empty. Benches sit unneeded, unused. The warm autumn sun feels wonderful. Basking in it, I begin to relax.

A nun crosses the square walks right up to me and asks, "Are you going to be here much longer?"

I look at my watch. It's not five-thirty yet. "Yes, I should be here another half hour."

"I need a nap and wonder if you will please watch over me as I sleep. It will be just a catnap, but if you need to leave before I awaken just shake my shoulder."

"Sure." With that she pulls her habit around her ankles and stretches out on the adjoining bench. I return to my reverie. Bourbon Street had been more than I expected. I wasn't ready for that young girl with the boozy breath bumping into me on the sidewalk, putting one arm around my shoulder while her other went south, asking if I wanted a little fun. I got away fast and checked my wallet. It was still there. I didn't expect so many bars would have their doors open to the sidewalk, with Dixieland bands playing. The French Market had been a disappointment, a complete washout compared to the one I saw Ingrid Bergman stroll through in *Saratoga Trunk*. There were just a few quiet stalls displaying some fruit and vegetables but no merchants crying, "Frrrresh Straaawberrries," "Praaalines," or "Frrresh Fish." But the Market's position right on top of the levee, with the enormous Mississippi River flowing by so rapidly, was exciting. I could clearly see how much higher the river is than the city streets. With that much water out there moving so fast, the Market and the whole city seem balanced on the edge of disaster. It chilled me to think of how that water, misdirected, could destroy this beautiful place in the twinkling of an eye.

"Hey, Mister, are you savin' that seat?" I wake from my reverie and look up to see a husky young man with a big boyish smile standing in front of me pointing to my bench.

"No." He sits down closer to me than I expect. Remembering the boozy girl, I wonder what he is up to. I look around the Square. I am the only man in a business suit. I am the only man with a tie. I am a target! I should have left my tie and coat at the hotel and come here in an open shirt.

"Thank you. Where do you hail from, Mister?"

"I'm from Virginia."

"Watcha doing down here?"

"I'm here for a shipbuilding standardization meeting."

"Sounds pretty complicated to me. What do you standardize?"

"Shipboard equipment and building methods. We are just beginning on a long road of work."

"I jess came in off a long road. Haven't been back here since last spring. I like to keep moving. Jess look at all them pigeons out there. Jess right for eating." He continues. "My Pa and I used to shoot pigeons even smaller than those, roast them on the spit. I can taste 'em now. Humm-humm, their little breasts are so good."

I've eaten squab but never ratty city pigeons, and this young man's enthusiasm for pigeons in the square, consuming leftovers from humans, escapes me.

He goes on talking, asking specifically where I am from. I tell him Newport News. I finally guess he is harmless and just wants to talk to somebody. He remembers Newport News and tells me about sleeping overnight there on a picnic table in a park and being wakened by some picnickers who invited him to eat lunch with them. He remembers how pretty the girls were and how good their food was. As we talk, nearby benches begin to fill. He still puzzles me. If he is homeless, he is the best-dressed homeless man I have seen, sitting there in a spotless white T-shirt and clean khakis, looking as if he had just walked off a college campus or out of a laundromat.

His gaze wanders from the delectable pigeons to some delectable young girls who have filled a nearby bench. He stands up and with great deliberation, begins to pull the bottom of his T-shirt out of his trousers. Then, very slowly, he pulls his shirt off. Dropping it on the bench, he yawns and stretches. Muscles seem to pop out in all directions. Then he raises his arms in front of him tensing his muscles again, spreads his legs, and does a couple windmills. They see him. He looks at them and smiles. They smile back. There is some giggling over there. He does have a winning grin I must admit, all boyish and full of innocence. There is no question about that. With his mop of sandy hair, he probably looks like the boy those girls hope will move in next door. But after his triumph with the girls and some more smiles in their direction, his conversation returns to the pigeons. I think I understand him now, get the drift of his intentions. He must be hungry and hoping I will take him to dinner. Men in suits can do that, but it doesn't appeal to me at all.

"What's up with the nun on the next bench?" he asks.

"I don't know. She asked me to watch after her while she took a catnap. I've never seen a nun take a nap on a park bench before. She was so casual about it when she asked me, I figure she must do it all the time."

"Well, inside every nun's heart there has been a wish for Prince Charming to wake her with a kiss. Think she would mind if I did it," he asks with that big smile filling his face.

"No, I don't think you should do that."

As I am talking, the nun sits up, stretches and comes over and sits on the other side of me. This is getting interesting.

Stretching and yawning, she says, "That was just what I needed. I couldn't go back there this afternoon nor am I going back for dinner."

"What's *there*," I ask.

"St. Catherine's School. I got angrier than I should have this afternoon. I am not always a good nun. I did something I shouldn't have done. I am not ready to go back. Say, are you two going to find dinner? I would like to join you if I may. I've got money. I can go Dutch."

"Sounds good to me," the husky young man says. "This gentleman jess arrived from Virginia. If we go, I want to take him to the Old Iron Pot on Camp Street for a real New Orleans dinner. OK?"

Now I am perplexed, but I wouldn't miss dinner at the Old Iron Pot with these two for the world. I hear myself saying, "Yes, by all means, let's go!"

"Just one request," the nun says, "We must walk down Royal Street. I want to look at the antique shops. It's right on the way." The nun raises her hand as we pass the third antique dealer. "I must go in here." We follow her. The shop is stuffed with junky-looking antiques of every kind. She disappears. Then a call comes from a distant corner, "Hey, Mister, come here." I find her in a dark corner examining a three-quarter sized statue of Diana. She is leaning over, running her hand over the white marble. "Give me your hand," she says "You've got to feel this polished marble." She takes my hand. I bend down, feel her breath on the back of my neck. She runs my hand over Diana's hips then moves it higher under her left breast. I pull my hand away and head out the door. She comes out a few minutes later, "I'm sorry, Mister, I wanted you to feel her stomach when I lost my balance."

"Hey, my stomach is growling," the young man moans. "Let's get going."

We continue down Royal. The nun pauses in front of other shop windows but we do not go in. We finally get to Canal Street, cross it, and reach Camp Street. There, ahead, is the sign of the Old Iron Pot.

I am surprised to find a very clean, brightly lit, airy restaurant set within sandblasted brick walls of an old building. The raw unfinished brick gives a certain aura of age and authenticity. But the big surprise is the hostess. She drops her menus on the desk and with outstretched arms rushes to us flinging them about the husky young man. "Jules, you are back. God, how we have missed you. Are you here for the winter?"

Jules hugs her and says, "I hope so. You're lookun beautiful, Sara Ann, and you feel even better." I notice his left hand caressing her perfect little fanny and her hand is busy on his too. "Now how about a table by the fountin?" Sara Ann leads us to a small table next to a gurgling fountain. She gives Jules one more long kiss, hands us the menus, and returns to her station.

Jules leans over the table confiding, "Even though this place is owned by Rose and staffed by women, it has the best crawfish gumbo étouffée and the best bread pudding with bourbon sauce in town. It's where New Orleaner's come to eat. I hope you will order them. Gumbo is New Orleans, Mister Virginia. You gotta have some before you leave town."

All the time he has been talking, the nun has been rubbing her napkin on her lips, looking at Jules. He finally gets it, and wipes the cherry-red lipstick off his mouth.

As he finishes, a waitress noiselessly arrives behind him and starts rubbing the back of his neck with her pencil. "Mary Sue, that must be you, you old sweetie."

"Sure enough, Hon. It's me." and with that she plants her kiss on his smiling lips.

"Hope you are going to stay a while." Jules stands up and hugs her, and I see her too checking the firmness of Jules's butt. Then she pulls back and asks, "You want your usual?"

"Yes and for this gentleman from Virginia, too."

The nun orders, catches my eye, and says "I want to see your hand." I can't make sense of her request but figure what can I lose? Then I remember the softness of her hand as she was running mine over Diana and prepare myself. At least this time she won't be breathing on the back of my neck.

But I am not prepared. For the first time, I see her beautiful hazel eyes looking intently into mine. She turns my hand over, palm up, and runs a finger over it. I quiver. "I used to read palms, and I have wanted to read yours since I saw you this afternoon. I won't tell you the bad, only the good. All right? Oh, what a lifeline. You will have obstacles, many obstacles, along the way, but you will have a long, long life. You will have love, too, one love for all of that life." Her finger traces other lines in my palm, and I see her face changing from questioning to fear, then peace. She releases my hand, looks at me and says. "I will say no more." My heart is pounding and I am overly warm.

"Hey, sweets, I've got a palm, too. How 'bout a reading?" Jules says, holding out his muscular hand. She takes it, studies it, brings her napkin to her face to hide a smile, then continuing her examination, she begins to giggle. Squeezing his hand with both of hers, she falls into uncontrollable laughter. Heads turn to see a laughing nun holding a young man's hand. Jules sees them and withdraws his hand. But before he can collect himself, another waitress is stroking the back of his ear with her fore finger.

"Hon, I have missed you. Hope you aren't going to walk away again without saying hello to little Bulah Jane."

"Bulah, let me look at you. Why you are prettier than a Louisiana sunrise. Of course I been thinking of you every night jes before I go to sleep and in my dreams, too. Are you ready for a little attention?" Jules stands, pulls Bulah Jane hard against his straight body, gives her a deep one, and releases her.

Good God, I wonder, has he bedded all of them? I look at him sitting there with a smile of sublime happiness on his boyish face as he munches a hot roll.

The crawfish étouffée is almost too rich to eat, but I finish the last morsel and the bread pudding with steaming hot black coffee is like nothing I have ever put my tongue to.

A ravishingly beautiful blonde walks out the kitchen door, unbuttoning her chef's coat, revealing a black sequined tank tucked into skin-tight jeans. Wow! She walks to our table and commands, "Jules, Hun, you get up for Mama Rose."

Jules stands up and she puts one on him that stops conversation. Her right hand, too, is down there checking his buns. "You know, Hon, we got a lot of catching up to do and those buns of yours need a lot more time in Mama Rose's kitchen. Now, this evening's dinner for you and your friends is on the house. Your old job's here too. You can start tonight, providing you do what you did before."

"Hon, jess wait till my guests finish an I'll be back." Then Rose saunters back into the kitchen. "She owns the place," he explains. "I used to work here and I like it."

I understand that statement but am puzzled by Rose's condition for returning.

"Jules, what did she mean by 'What you did before'?" I ask.

"Oh, its nuttin. They like me to work back there with my shirt off. That's all. It's a good situation, working with these loving girls every night. Can't beat it. Well it was nice meeting you and having dinner with you. I'm headin' to the kitchen. If you eat here again, come to the kitchen and say hello. I'll be there." Enjoyed your company. I need to get started. Goodnight."

We say goodbye, and I ask the nun if I can take her back to her school. She thinks it would be better to return alone and we part. It's then I realize she didn't bow her head, cross herself, pause, or even close her eyes before eating. No devotion! I give her a quarter of a block and then follow her. She crosses Canal, walks four blocks up Canal, and turns right into Bourbon Street.

I have to move fast to keep sight of her in the crowd. She stops to talk to a man who is leaning against a building. He straightens up, nuzzles her, and slides his arm around her. They walk to the end of the building and disappear. I catch up and find a staircase going up the end of the building with a dim light at the top. I see him just going in the door. Unashamedly I cross the street, look up at the second story window. A light comes on. The nun appears in the window to pull the shade down when he reaches her. Off comes her habit revealing a black lace teddy.

The next evening I am bone weary following a day of boring negotiations. I head for my room after a long Scotch at the bar. Just as the elevator doors are closing a middle-aged man and young woman jump in laughing and talking excitedly, obviously headed for fun.

I wonder where the party is. She turns and looks at me. There, again, are those beautiful hazel eyes. Quickly, she turns away and snuggles her escort. I look at the floor number display eager to leave, wondering who my "nun" will be tomorrow.

The Caregiver

M. L. Kline

When Clare called her mother with the test results, Alva's reaction was one of indignation.

"What am I? Too old and senile for the doctor himself to tell me I have pneumonia?"

"Mother, when he ordered the x-rays and blood work, you told him to call me if they found anything. Remember? Besides, it's a mild case. There's no need to worry."

"Well, he let me suffer with it long enough. Did he think I'd die and save him the trouble of calling in a prescription?"

"He's a good doctor, Mother. He doesn't want you to die."

"Probably the only one who doesn't," mumbled Alva.

Clare took a deep breath before asking, "So, how did you sleep last night?"

"Sleep? If you can call it that, I slept. Sat up all night with the African on my shoulders. That's how I slept."

"Mother, you mean the afghan."

"That's what I said. Never spent a more miserable night."

Clare could picture her mother, asleep in the chair, her head falling forward, then snapping back as she came awake again. On her lap would be pieces of discount brand tissues, torn apart by Alva as she watched television.

Always, after Alva's visits to Clare's home, the children and Clare's husband would gather up debris that she left behind. There were peppermint wrappers, cake crumbs, shredded tissues, address labels torn from magazines. The family threatened constantly to bring it to Alva's attention, but Clare always held them off.

"Don't," she'd say. "You'll only hurt her feelings. Mother isn't really aware of doing those things."

So Clare resorted to snatching up the bits of trash herself, from the house and car, from church pews, from doctors' offices. She found herself slamming them into receptacles with the irritation of someone who had just awakened to a lawn covered with discarded beer cans. Her anger turned to shock when she discovered her mother deliberately hiding candy wrappers under the sofa cushion.

Clare asked her friend, Marge, "Why does she do that? It drives me nuts."

Marge held a degree in psychology, had an ear for listening, and the good grace to keep things to herself.

"It could be a show of defiance," she said, "or a means of getting attention."

"That's crazy, Marge. I don't understand her. I really don't."

Leaving Alva's house a few days later, Clare cringed at her mother's words, flung out through a mouthful of Jell-O.

"Three days and I'm no better. What good's an antibody if it don't work?"

Clare fumbled with her coat buttons, twisting one from its threads as she headed down the front steps.

"Mother, you're eighty-two years old. Even young children don't recover that quickly. It takes time!"

"Well, I don't have much of that, I can tell you!" shouted Alva, tossing a paper napkin over the porch railing. A ringing telephone pulled her back inside, while Clare listened to her mother's voice evolve into a maddening sweetness.

"Oh, hello, Mary! Yes . . . doing much better, thanks. My daughter's taking care of me. Good care. Just brought me some delicious lime Jell-O."

Clare shoved the detached button into her coat pocket. Alva's immediate response to the offered dessert had been, "I hate the taste of lime. . . ."

She called Marge as soon as she got home.

"She'll say these nice things about me to other people, Marge, but never to me. I get a negative reaction to everything I do for her."

"I think it's just hard for her to voice affection or praise, Clare, so she goes about it in this roundabout way. I know it must be confusing for you."

"You've got that last part right. And she's always angry, always complaining. With everyone else, she's all sunshine and roses. Most of the time, I feel like I'm dealing with Jekyll and Hyde."

"Well, I imagine she resents her loss of independence. She uses you as a sounding board for her anger and frustration. You're all she has, Clare . . . and there are ways of dealing with this behavior. You might want to consider professional help. . . ."

Clare's mouth opened to speak, then closed again. Her fingers had peeled back a seam of wallpaper in the kitchen.

"I'll call you later, Marge. Thanks."

The phone rang as soon as Clare hung up. It was Alva.
"I'm going to take a bath now, in case you try to call me."
"All right, Mother, but try not to get chilled."
"Why? I'm half dead now. Might as well finish off the other half."
Exasperated, Clare slid the receiver down and pressed it against the tightness in her chest. She could feel the vibration of her mother's voice against her breastbone.
"Clare? Are you listening?"
"Yes. Yes, I am. I was thinking . . . maybe we should get a safety rail installed for your bathtub. I worry that you might fall. . . ."
"Safety rail? You've got to be kidding! All this money I put out for medicines and you think I need to spend more? Forget it. Piece of foolishness. If I'm going to throw money away, I'll take a nice trip. Mary's daughter just sent her to the Pinocchios. All expenses paid."
"Mother, it's the Poconos."
"I know that. That's what I said."
"Well, I can't afford to send you on a vacation. I just want to get you a safety rail. You could fall in that tub and lay there for God knows how long."
"Yeah, and I could get hit by a truck, too," said Alva, and hung up.

Alva's words stirred up old memories. Years ago, her mother really had been hit by a truck. Clare was eight months pregnant when she got the call telling her that Alva was still conscious after being struck and thrown into the air. She had landed on the grassy edge of a public park.

A stranger told Clare, "She gave me this number. Insisted I call you. I think her leg's broke, and she's got a bad bump on her head. Amazing. She musta flew twenty feet in the air. Shoulda been killed."

Clare rushed to the hospital, finding Alva badly bruised, with a concussion and a locked kneecap requiring surgery. Alva's first words to her were, ". . . my slip."

"What do you mean, Mother? You slipped?"
"Didn't slip . . . truck hit me."
"I know, I know. But you're going to be all right."

Alva raised her head and whispered to Clare, "Safety pin . . ."
"What safety pin?"
"Had on . . . slip . . . with safety pin."
Clare understood perfectly. Alva had broken the rule she often repeated to her daughter, that you never went out unless you wore your best underwear. You never knew when you'd be in an accident. And there was Alva, more afraid of being seen in her faulty underclothes than she was of broken bones and head injuries.

Clare had scolded her.

"Mother, you could have been killed. This is no time to worry over the fact that your slip was held together with a pin!"

On that day, Clare had realized how close she'd come to losing her mother. The knot in her stomach was like a labor contraction. And she remembered how, when she looked down at Alva in that hospital bed, she saw tears in her mother's eyes for the first time in her life. Clare quickly offered a box of tissues, but Alva turned her face to the wall and said, "You go on home now."

Later on, Marge tried to comfort Clare by saying, "She pushes you away because she needs you so much. . . ."

Clare paced the kitchen, clutching both arms, holding onto herself. Life with Alva was one of constant frustration. She never knew the right words to say, or how to please her, or how to connect. She wished she could say, "Okay, then. Go take a bath. Go fall down in the tub. If you break a bone, we'll deal with it. It's up to you."

But she couldn't. She wanted to make things better, not worse.

She turned toward the liquor cabinet, hoping to find something that would calm her nerves. She'd rejected her doctor's idea of an occasional tranquilizer. Perhaps a little drink would work just as well. There was an opened bottle of vodka, so she filled half a juice glass and added ice. Then, because it tasted so badly, she added root beer and stirred it with a fork. She wondered what Marge would have to say about that.

Clare had filled and drained the glass three times when the phone rang. She was sitting on the floor, her head resting against the refrigerator, amazed at the lightness of her body. It was as if something had gently pulled back the wires that were trying to choke her. It was a nice sensation.

Four rings later, she was finally upright, one hand braced against a wall, the other struggling with the receiver.

Alva's voice was shaking with irritation.

"Well, it's about time. You never called to make sure I'd gotten out of the tub."

"Sorry," said Clare. "I was . . . somewhere else."

"Are you catching a cold? You sound like you are. What am I supposed to do if you get sick? I can't take care of your family. I can hardly take care of myself."

"I wouldn't expect you to do anything, Mother."

"You don't understand. But mark my words, you will when you get old."

Clare steadied herself by hanging onto the refrigerator door handle. She raised her eyes heavenward and spoke to the ceiling.

". . . I'm not sure I'll live long enough to get old."

Alva was in the middle of a coughing spell and never heard. As soon as she was able, she told Clare, "Well, I decided. You call those Medicare people and see if they cover safety rails. When I'm gone, you can yank it out and use it for yourself."

"Mother, they don't cover things like that. I just want to buy you one."

"You mean to tell me they pay for those silly scooters, but won't let me have a rail? Mary had one of those things once. Pushed a chair into her curio. Broke the glass and all her crystal. Piece of foolishness."

Clare digested this news for the umpteenth time, telling Alva, "Let's just be thankful you don't need a scooter, Mother. You get around just fine."

"Who knows what I'll need before this is over? That's why I save my money, so you don't have to spend yours. Lord knows, I don't want to be a burden."

"Mother . . ."

"What now?"

"I love you."

"Well . . . all right then. But don't get me one of those cheap plastic things. I want stainless steel. Holds up better."

"I'll try to find a sturdy one," said Clare. "I'll even throw in a new bathmat."

"Not unless it's a Rubbermaid, you won't. The rest is junk. Falls apart on you."

"I'll make sure it doesn't fall apart on you, Mother," promised Clare, pressing with one finger a portion of liquid glue into the opened seam of wallpaper.

The Monkey Man

D.. S. Lliteras

I wanted to see his little black nose poke through the partially opened door when I came home from work in the morning, but I wasn't expecting it. My old boy was very sick. He almost died of renal failure at the animal hospital. He'd been home from intensive care for three days.

I went to my study and saw him lying near my desk where he watched me write eight novels. I knelt down to touch him. "Smokey?" He was as hard as a stone. "Smokey. Oh, God." I whispered into his ear. "I love you, Smokey. I love you. You're my boy. You'll always be my boy." Then I buried my face in his furry neck and cried.

The scent of the hospital's kennel competed with the scent of death.

I heard my wife stirring about upstairs. I knew she was worried about Smokey. I knew her sorrow would be as intense as mine. I massaged the back of Smokey's left ear.

"How's he doing?" she whispered anxiously as she approached me.

I hesitated. Once the words were said, it was final. "He's dead."

Her explosive yelp brought me to my feet. We embraced. We burst into tears.

"I fell asleep," she said. "He was alright three o'clock this morning."

"What happened?"

"I slept down here with him until midnight—until he started roaming the house and lying in his different spots like he always did. He seemed alright. So . . . so, I went upstairs to get a couple of hours of sleep. He was alright when I came down at three o'clock to check up on him. He was alright."

"Was he breathing heavily?"

"Yes. But he was alright. I petted him and talked to him, then I went upstairs to get a couple of hours of sleep. But I overslept!"

"I'm glad." I knelt down and stroked his back. "I think he knew how much we loved him, how much we wanted him to live. He didn't want to disappoint us. But he was so sick. So sweet. I think he waited until he could die alone." I burst into tears. "He was so damn sweet."

"I know, I know." She knelt down and caressed me.

"It's going to be hard not seeing him again." I inhaled to control my emotions. "This . . . this forever is the hardest thing to take."

"I'm going to miss him." She stood up, shuddered, and went to the kitchen to get away from herself. This reminded me of Smokey waking up and shaking himself from head to toe, then stepping away from his spot as if he were walking away from slumber.

I always enjoyed his little activities. They were a constant source of wonder. He yawned to express excitement and he cocked his head to one side to express curiosity. He breathed heavily when he was happy and danced in a small circle to convey his joy. He usually nudged my arm with his wet nose to gain my attention, but sometimes he whimpered until he heard me say, "Hey there, Monkey Man." He knew I always had time for him.

Black fur covered his head and back, his tail and both flanks; red fur covered his forehead and chest, his rear end and his legs. He was a happy creature with dark eyes and a red tongue, an intelligent being with a gentle temperament, despite his one hundred and twenty pounds.

Tears streamed down my cheeks as I stroked the side of Smokey's face. The scent of feces and urine strengthened death's presence.

My wife entered the study. "I made coffee. Do you want anything to eat?"

"No. Just coffee."

She knelt beside Smokey. "He needs to be buried." She petted him. "I'm so sorry, honey."

"For what?"

"He loved you so."

"He loved you, too."

"He was your boy."

"That's not true."

"Come on. Let's have some coffee."

I followed her into the kitchen.

The cheese Danish tasted like soap and the coffee burned like acid. But I ate and drank because I didn't know what else to do with my grief.

My wife got up from the table and poured the water from Smokey's plastic bowl down the sink.

"What are you doing?" I asked.

"It's making me crazy."

"What?"

"Everywhere I look, there's Smokey."

I wanted to tell her that I liked seeing Smokey's presence. But I wanted to respect her pain as well.

She cleared out a kitchen drawer full of Smokey's personal effects—two leashes and a comb, a thick medical record and a jar of heartworm pills, an array of empty prescription bottles and his vitamins.

I went to my study and I sat on the floor beside him and studied his face while my wife gathered up what was left of his life: toys, balls, throw rugs, food, shampoo—he filled the four corners of our home.

After a while, I went into the laundry room and returned with Smokey's comb, his nail clipper, and a pair of scissors. I combed out a bunch of hair from his back and put it in a small plastic bag I found in my desk drawer. My boy hated having his toenails clipped, so I apologized to him before I took hold of his left front paw and clipped one of his nails. Then I snipped off a short length of hair from the tip of his tail with the scissors.

I placed the tail hair and the toenail in the plastic bag and went into the garage, where I placed the bag, the comb, and the nail clipper into an old cookie tin. Then I hid the tin in the garage. I planned to store the reliquary in my bedroom bureau.

I went back to my study and sat beside Smokey for a long time.

"Honey. We've got to do something about Smokey."

"Later," I said.

"It's not healthy leaving him like that."

"Later."

"He's got to be buried."

"I said later, damn it."

She left the study and went upstairs.

I was ashamed of my anger, but I was more disturbed by the speed in which she was eliminating Smokey's presence. I stood up, went into the living room, and discovered several cardboard boxes full of Smokey's things. I closed the lid of the nearest box, picked it up, and took it into the garage. When I returned for another box, my wife was standing in the living room with a sheet and bedspread.

"I'm taking his stuff into the garage," I said.

"That's nice."

"Don't throw anything away."
"I won't."
"What's that?"
"I thought it would be nice to wrap him in a clean sheet."
"And the bedspread?"
"I thought we could use this to carry him outside."
I shook my head. "No. He's too heavy for that."
"Then how are we going to—"
"Wait. Let me think."
"We've got to—"
"I said let me think." I took the second box into the garage before my irritation strengthened into anger; she followed me.

As soon as I set the box on the floor, I opened an aluminum storage cabinet and found an old shower curtain I'd saved. "We'll slip this under him and drag him outside through the back door. The plastic will make it easier."

"Okay." She was relieved.

We slipped the folded shower curtain under his stiff body.

I didn't want to disturb him; his right leg was tucked underneath his chest. I didn't want to hurt him; his weak hips were common among German Shepherds.

We lifted the opposite corners of the plastic curtain and dragged the boy across the study, through the back door, and into the yard: I pulled and she steered. I refrained from issuing too many orders to avoid bickering during our physically demanding procession to the northwest corner of the backyard.

After we reached our destination, we sat down on the nearby cement bench to rest. A privacy fence and a dogwood tree shaded this corner of the property.

This was a place where I wrote during the spring and summer, while Smokey roamed and sniffed and vied for my attention by teasing me with that dirty ball in his mouth. That ball he thought I wanted, that dirty old beautiful ball he loved to play with so much, sat lifelessly in the middle of the backyard. I held back my tears.

I stood up and approached the miniature door, which led to the house's crawl space. I opened the door and took out a shovel, a mattock, and a rake.

"Can I help?"
"No, honey." I gathered the tools and went to the intended grave site.
"I want to help."
"Digging a grave is heavy work. I don't want you to hurt your back."

"My back's fine."

"I want to do this. Can you understand that?" I leaned the mattock and shovel against the dogwood tree. "I want to do this."

"I want to help," she whispered.

I twirled the upright rake a couple of times before I looked into her green eyes. "I'm sorry. I'm being selfish."

"I understand."

"We'll take turns."

"Okay. I'll be right back."

I raked the leaves into a mound, then I used the point of the shovel to cut a five-by-three foot rectangular outline into the black dirt. The shovel bit easily into the soft topsoil.

My wife returned with the sheet and bedspread.

I stopped digging. "What are you doing?"

"I'm going to cover him."

"Don't. Please. He's going to be covered forever."

"Alright." She laid the sheet and bedspread beside Smokey, then sat on the bench.

I dug slowly. I thought about my boy.

Smokey was always with me when I did yard work. If I was raking in the autumn, he'd scatter the leaves; if I was mowing in the summer, he'd be in the way. I didn't mind.

After the ground became hard, I had to use the mattock more than the shovel. It was a sad labor of love and sweat and dirt.

My wife grew impatient. I delayed her assistance by asking her for a glass of water. Then I broke the ground for her with the mattock.

I traded the idle shovel for the glass of water when she returned.

"Don't hurt your back."

"I won't."

I helped her into the grave and noted her reaction to the rough inner earth, the protruding roots, and the multicolored dirt stratas. The grave was dark and cool and alien to her. She dug steadily as I drank my water.

She did not have great stamina, but she had great heart. As soon as the dirt grew hard, I stood up and grabbed the mattock before she thought to reach for it.

"What do you think you're doing?" she asked.

"I need to break that ground."

She glanced at the mattock. "I'm digging."

"You'll hurt yourself with this." I extended my hand to her. "Please. Take a break."

She released the shovel and allowed me to assist her out of the grave. Then I gave her my empty glass and asked her for more water. This became our routine until the grave was dug several feet—until my wife approached the edge of the grave as I aimed the raised mattock before taking the next swing.

"It's deep enough, honey."

"No, it's not," I said.

"Honey, please—"

"Damn it, woman, leave me alone!" I swung the mattock hard into the clay and pried open a large chunk of ground. I was forced to dislodge a big clump of clay that stuck to the inside flat of the mattock's blade and pitch it out of the grave. "Sorry. I'll stop as soon as I level out the bottom."

"Good. I'll cover him."

"Don't."

She remained silent despite my behavior.

Once I had the bottom leveled, I tossed the shovel and mattock toward the dogwood tree, climbed out of the grave, and sat on the cement bench beside my wife. "Are you alright?"

"Are you?"

"I know I've been impossible."

"I'm not operating too well myself."

"God, I'm going to miss him."

"Me, too."

We sat for a long time. I was tired. But I wasn't about to say that to my wife.

"Are you ready?"

"What's the rush?" I said, irritably.

"I want to get this over with."

"Well, I don't."

A strong silence separated our differences. She compromised by waiting, and I compromised by not making her wait too long.

I stood up. "Come on. Let's get it done."

We dragged Smokey near the foot of the grave.

I jumped in. "Be careful, honey. I'm going to pull him toward me, but I don't want you holding his weight. Just let him drop over the edge, okay?"

"You be careful."

"I will, I will. Ready?"

"Yes."

I pulled my corners of the shower curtain and guided the length of his body past the edge; his weight quickly followed.

"Let go," I said, realizing she was about to ignore my instructions.

She let go. I dragged him into his final resting place.

He looked peaceful. I stood there for a long time and prayed silently to myself.

"Are you ready?" she asked.

"Wait." I knelt beside the boy and kissed him. Then I scratched the back of his ear for the last time before whispering to him. "I love you, Smokey. Don't be afraid of the thunder and lightning, Monkey Man."

My wife handed me the sheet and bedspread as soon as I stood up. "Thanks." I carefully draped the sheet over him, then placed the bedspread on top of that. I kept folding and tucking until I felt my wife's growing impatience, then I climbed out.

We stood over the grave for a few contemplative moments, then I scooped up some dirt with the shovel and gently poured it over the boy. I handed the shovel to my wife and she performed the same ritual. Then I took the shovel from her and started filling in the grave. I wanted to stop and peek under the sheet and bedspread, but the impulse subsided after all the fabric disappeared.

We took turns with the shovel.

When we were almost finished, I set the shovel aside and danced on the grave to pack down the dirt. I danced and I danced and I danced.

"Honey. Honey. I think that's enough."

I kept dancing until fatigue dissolved my trance. Then I picked up the shovel and spread the last layer of dirt, smoothed it out, and raked the leaves over the top. "It looks pretty good, doesn't it?"

"Yes, it does."

I marked the head of the grave with a large grey stone and the foot of the grave with a smaller stone. I was pleased when my wife offered me a votive candle and a book of matches.

"Thanks." I placed the candle on the large rough stone and lit it.

"That's beautiful."

"Yeah." I tossed the spent match away. "I'm sorry."

"For what?"

"For you having to put up with me."

"Don't be ridiculous."

I picked up the shovel, the mattock, and the rake and stored them in the crawl space underneath the house.

"Are you hungry?"

I lied. "Yes."

"Why don't you take a shower while I make us something to eat."

"Okay."

We went inside, leaving Smokey in the company of a flickering candle.

I took a shower and, afterwards, watched my wife make dinner for a while. Then I got up from the kitchen table and went into my study where I felt:

    the emptiness, filling
     the place where my dog
     died in his sleep.

The Left Ascension

D.. S. Lliteras

The long, hot summer melted his consciousness and dissipated his spirit. He wanted to feel other than day old, but the need to scratch behind his left armpit reinforced his stagnant disposition.

He lounged on a broken lawn chair nestled within the crack of two buildings that was almost too narrow to be called an alley. He stared into his mug full of cheap rye and cold coffee.

Unwashed body; dirty t-shirt. Uncombed hair; clouded mind. Unshaven face; bankrupt soul. He was broke and broken and spiritually immobilized.

What happened?

He thought he was enlightened; he thought he was pure until he fell, or failed, or sinned: utterly and completely, which banished him from his religious practice.

He gulped down half the muddy liquid, then grimaced.

You egomaniac.

He gulped down the rest of the drink, including the bitter dregs on the bottom. Then he stared into his empty mug and went blank. This was a long way from his former meditative way of life: zen life, monastic life, everyday life, no life.

Somebody was playing Brahms' Piano Concerto number 2.

Odd. Such beauty in an intolerably ugly world.

He sighed.

He was deluded when he lived in the peace of a constant false joy, in the certainty of a here-and-now existence. Monastic life was as much a lie as secular life.

Where did that leave him?

Lost. Ignorant. Trapped in the eternal cycle of existence. Asking questions and getting answers that required faith.

He stood up and hurled the mug at a brick wall and watched it shatter. This empty act was as devoid of meaning as his life and his faith.

All because of what. What? What!

"A woman. Me! All that discipline, all those spiritual years destroyed because of an erection! You knew she was married. You understood the moral tightrope you were walking on! You knew you were heading for spiritual suicide! And you knew you were destroying two other people as well!"

Somebody leaned out of their second-floor window and called down to him. "Come on, man, give me a break. It's seven thirty in the morning, and Saturday is my only day to sleep late."

"I'm sorry." He waved at the man. "It won't happen again. I promise."

The man closed the window unimpressed by the apology.

He felt foolish. Paranoid. Self-indulgent. He couldn't face the world. His spiritual endeavors kept proving to him the universal lack of truth.

He went down a flight of stairs, which led to his windowless, basement apartment.

He sat down at his kitchenette table and stared at the Colt 38 Special. The black revolver was pointed at the refrigerator.

Who told him it was dangerous to embark on a spiritual path?

He picked up the revolver. There was one bullet hidden among six chambers. He pressed the barrel against his right temple and pulled the trigger.

Click. He felt nothing. He pulled the trigger again. Click. He felt ashamed.

He placed the revolver on the table and released it undramatically.

What now? Why this reprieve?

He didn't want it. He was tired of thinking, of meditation, of contemplation, of himself—of life.

He grabbed the revolver and pointed the barrel at his chest.

If I can't kill the mind, then I'll kill the heart.

He pulled the trigger. Click. Then insistently: click!

He dropped the revolver on the table, stood up, and kicked the chair aside.

"No, damn it! No!"

Or had it been yes all his life?

He believed in Christianity when he believed. He believed in Pantheism when he believed. In Buddhism, in karma, in atheism. In past lives, reincarnation, shamanism, and zen. In the unity of the universe, in the here and now. He believed in it all, and in nothing.

He snatched the revolver from the table and pulled the trigger as soon as the barrel touched his abdomen. Click.

A wave of calm swept across him, then he felt sick. There was no energy left for thoughts or feelings: for bargains or covenants or justifications, for theological hairsplitting or philosophical inquires or syllogistic conclusions. He was an angel standing on the point of a needle.

He clinically inserted the barrel into his mouth and pulled the trigger. Click.

A bead of perspiration burned his right eye. "Damn."

He rubbed his eye with the heel of his left hand. Then he threw the revolver across the room, stumbled backwards, and crashed against a chest of drawers. When he regained his equilibrium, he was startled by the object he saw.

Two-thirds of it gleamed like a piece of gold and the other third of it glared like tarnished silver. The bullet was cradled in an empty ashtray on the bureau.

He'd forgotten to insert the bullet!

Hysteria assaulted him. His crazed laughter ended with tears.

"Okay. This is good. Okay. You're stupid. Okay. There's a God."

The realization struck his soul.

"Is this spiritual poverty?"

There was no intense light. No euphoria.

"By disregarding my life, have I found it again?"

Life planted him firmly on two feet. There was nothing to be afraid of, no matter what direction the arrow of consciousness pointed. Into nothing or everlasting life were the same thing and . . . and was he deluded?

"It doesn't matter. I don't care. I won't seek—no—I can't give it a definition."

For the first time in months, he wondered what the hell he was doing drinking rye in the morning.

He took off his dirty clothes, jumped into the shower, and whistled like a bird without a tune.

Summer 1956

Jim Meehan

Dusk comes early to the hollows under the Blue Ridge Mountains, even in the long, bright days of July. The shimmering sun is partially hidden behind the trees on the ridges by late afternoon and long shadows stretch down the mountain, reaching across the narrow country roads to give at least the illusion of a cool darkness approaching.

We were still playing baseball on the dusty farm field, but I could see that the fence in the far outfield was growing dim as the light failed.

"O.K., that's all for today," I announced.

"One more inning! Just one more!" yelled Billy.

I pulled off my Dodgers cap and wiped the sweat from my forehead with the front of the sleeveless red t-shirt.

"One more, you sumbitch? You were yelling to quit two innings ago when you were ahead!" I taunted Billy.

Billy laughed and his teeth glowed white as the dim light closed in on us.

"Come on, Jim, just one more inning."

"Not gonna happen. I don't want to have the first team to lose an outfielder to a bear out there in the dark. Anyways, we got you by three runs."

The kids were coming in from their positions and gathering around the rough pitcher's mound where I stood. Billy threw his glove on the ground, raising a whirl of dust at home plate, and kicked it along as he walked toward me. The rest of his team unfolded from the rough benches and followed. I raised my right arm in front of me, palm open, and Billy grabbed it hard in an arm wrestler's grip.

"Good game, my man," he said.

"Good game, Billy."

We were a bunch of small town kids who tried to spend our afternoons on the ball field whenever we could during the summer.

Summer 1956

Twenty or so thirteen- and fourteen-year-olds, boys and a few girls who loved to play the game. The team line-ups changed from week to week, and the scores were often over twenty runs for each side as the endless innings passed.

We had no problems with adults, as our parents always knew where to find us. Old man Johnson, the owner of the field, had long ago relinquished the land to the ball players. He built the field for his kids decades ago, and it was passed along to each new generation of players. He came out sometimes to sit on a battered bench and watch the play; a weather-beaten old farmer in bib overalls and a straw hat. He never said much, just chewed tobacco and sometimes clapped his hands for a good play. We knew that one of his boys had not come home from the Second World War and we hoped our games brought back a few good memories for him.

The air began to show that hazy blue shadow that gave the mountains their name.

We walked in a noisy gaggle across the field toward the little country crossroads that was the center of our lives. A black Ford convertible, top down, roared out from town, and the driver popped the headlights on as the twilight closed in over the road. We heard a brief bit of Elvis wailing a rockabilly song as the Ford rapidly disappeared down the wooded road.

Rich, whose older brother Danny drove the convertible, started it and all of us boys joined in with the song.

"Train arriveeeeeed, sixteen, uh, coaches long."

The girls covered their ears and ran ahead of us with a burst of giggles.

"That long black train, got ma baby and gonnnnnnne."

More cries and complaints from the girls.

Rich yelled, "Some people just don't appreciate good music," and the girls added a chorus of groans to their laughter.

We sauntered closer to the old general store at the crossroads and kids began to move off in different directions to go home.

"Good game, see ya tomorrow," as friends vanished into the darkening streets and tree-shrouded lanes on foot or bicycle.

I took off my cap and swatted Billy on the shoulder with it.

"Your team lost. Buy me a Coke," I said.

Billy swatted back and I ducked and weaved like a punch-drunk boxer.

"What? You think I'm rich or something?" he yelled.

"Naw, your momma's rich, so put it on her tab."

It was the same routine after every game, but we cherished these traditions.

There were seven of us left as we dropped our gloves on the steps, pushed through the screen door and into the dim light of the store. Old Bear, the huge black lab sprawled in the corner, raised his head. Bear gave a throaty bark that was half greeting and half warning to hold the noise down.

Mr. Suthard, the proprietor, gave us a grin and asked "Who won?"

"We did," we all chorused and laughed.

"Yeah, I reckon y'all did," he said.

Billy fed a couple of nickels into the big floor cooler and slid two Cokes out, passing one to me. Chilled condensation coated the heavy green bottle, and I rolled it across the back of my neck before I opened it. The other kids got their Cokes, and we headed back outside to stand on the porch. The old store was stuffy in the heat, and Mr. Suthard kept his radio tuned to the Grand Old Opry, which was just not compatible with our taste in music.

The wispy clouds over the mountains were turning red, and the sky brought a reflected brightness to the street. People, mostly couples, were walking along the sidewalks and looking into the few store windows. The little diner on the corner was beginning to fill up, dark silhouettes of customers passing in front of the brightly lit windows. A seemingly endless parade of old pickup trucks passed along the main street. Some were farm trucks chugging along at fifteen miles per and others sported chrome wheels and roared by in second gear with exhausts rumbling. I watched each one with envy. Lord, how I wanted a car, or a pickup, or a motorcycle—anything with an internal combustion engine and two or more wheels.

Sheriff Dupree leaned against his patrol car by the town square and glared at each of the loud vehicles as it passed, maintaining the speed limit by the severity of his look. A small town Saturday evening.

Two of the girls said their goodbyes and walked away together, leaving Billy and me, Rich, David, and Sarah. I noticed Sarah as she talked to David. The sunset colors gave her deep tan a rich luster, and her eyes gleamed from under her dark bangs. The little turned-up nose that had once been funny was now, well, cute. The baggy baseball jersey and cut off jeans did not quite hide a figure that was beginning to develop. This had not gone unnoticed by the boys in the gang. She took a swallow of her Coke and glanced my way, and I held her gaze until she turned away. She quickly brushed at her bangs and pushed her hair behind her ears, darting a glance back at me. I didn't understand what I was feeling, but I continued to look at her even though it was obviously making her uncomfortable.

The girls had begun showing up for the games last summer, and we boys had felt that "wish they would go away but hope they don't" attitude toward them. They cheered our home runs and double-plays and hooted when one of us dropped a fly ball. Eventually, the challenge went out—"Do you think you can do any better?" and soon they were playing and surprised us by playing well. This summer had been a little different. The kidding and wrestling around of the previous year seemed out of place when our female players started showing traces of make-up, tiny earrings, and training bras.

David started kidding around with Rich, and I turned to watch them playfully punching each other. Billy laughingly yelled encouragement to both of them. Sarah stepped closer to me then, and I turned toward her.

"Jim," she said, "those were the worst imitations of Elvis I have ever heard."

I looked at those bright blue eyes glowing in the sunset light and something crawled up out of my stomach and tried to choke me. I cleared my throat to keep from stammering.

"Aw, it was pretty good for a bunch of ballplayers. We're not the high school chorus here."

She laughed and brushed the hair back again.

"So, do you like Elvis?" she asked.

"Sure, but don't tell my folks. They think he's the devil himself."

"Yeah, so do mine, but I love his music. And he's soooo good looking."

Sarah had moved a little closer, and there was a hint of perfume to her as well as the dust and sweat.

"Did you see Elvis on the Steve Allen show?" I asked.

"Oh, yeah, and my parents went crazy. They actually made my little sister go to her room and not watch that part. I was lucky I got to see it."

"Yeah, I don't know how he does that bit with his knees," I said. I backed off and did an awkward version of the Elvis moves. Sarah brought her hands to her mouth to stifle the laughter.

"Hey, look at Elvis," Billy yelled, and the boys started in on me. Soon we were all doing Elvis or Jerry Lee or Buddy Holly.

The real darkness began to fall as we horsed around in front of the store, and Sarah announced that she had to get home. We broke it up then with the traditional "Good game" and gladiator handshakes all around. I stood the Coke bottles in the wooden crate on the porch, and we started for home. Sarah, Billy, and I passed the town square and walked down the lane. We stopped under one of the few streetlights in town and split up. Billy waved and started jogging toward his house, and I looked at Sarah.

"Can I walk you home, Sarah?"

She stepped closer and looked up at me. She gently bit her lower lip as she thought about my offer.

"Well, you're not Elvis, but I guess it'll be all right."

I laughed and looked at her under the weak light. I think we were both beginning to realize the power she would soon have but did not yet understand; the power to reduce strong young men to clowns begging for her approval and to break boys' hearts with a glance and a frown. It surely would come.

We walked slowly toward her house, replaying the highlights of the day's game. I finally started humming the Elvis tune. She smacked me on the arm and started running. I chased her all the way to her front door where the light spilled through the screen and onto the wooden porch. Her father looked out at us, and again I felt that nervous lump in my throat.

"Hi, Mr. Warren," I said.

Sarah's father squinted into the dark. "Hi, Sarah, Jim. I was starting to get a little concerned. It's getting dark out there, kids."

"We stopped for a Coke at the store, Dad," Sarah said.

"Well come on in the house, girl," her father replied.

Sarah turned to me. "Goodnight, Jim. Thanks for walking me home."

"Good game, Sarah. See you tomorrow."

"Good game, Jim. Tomorrow."

I stepped out into the street and glanced back at the house. Sarah was standing at the screen door looking out, a slender silhouette against the indoor light. Fireflies danced around the dark lawn, tiny golden comets filling the dark between us.

I walked home through the soft darkness and sang a little of the Elvis ballad, keeping the beat with my fist banging into my baseball glove. I imagined myself driving a black convertible, radio blaring out the song and Sarah sitting close beside me.

Maybe in a few years, maybe someday, maybe never. But it was nice to think about.

I turned up the driveway where my father stood in the dark, smoking; the glow of the ash made his fingers seem to float eerily red in the dark.

"Hi, son. Good game?"

"Yeah, Dad, real good game."

From a Distance, through the Foliage

Anne Meek

If there were more than five houses on our street, we might not take such an interest when one goes up for sale. But with only five, a For Sale sign is conspicuous, a banner of reproach casting doubt on the desirability of living on this street that is really a nice piece of real estate. So when the SOLD sign went up in front of the Taylor house, a certain heaviness lifted itself right out of our chests, replaced by relief and then, quickly, by curiosity about the new neighbors.

Within a few days, the grapevine yielded the news that a young couple had bought the house, that he was a professor of Russian studies at the university and that she had studied at the Sorbonne, had graduated from Radcliffe, lacked only her dissertation on a doctorate from another Ivy League school, and was a *haute cuisine* cook and *haute couture* model. Suddenly I felt twelve years old again, sharing gossip around the pool about the new girl in town, who was reported to have a lime green two-piece swimsuit and magenta polish on her toenails.

After the newcomers moved in, I made a loaf of sweet banana bread from my own recipe, and, when it had cooled, Tom and I carried it down the hill to welcome them. There they were in the driveway, approaching their car. He was short. She was tall . . . and so thin that the constricting power of her halter top met little resistance from her flesh. I dared not look at her below the chin for fear of seeing too much if the cloth should suddenly draw up to the measure of its own elastic. She evidently shared my fear, for she tugged first at one side of the halter and then the other. I didn't get a good look at her face, either, being so careful not to look below it; but I saw she was excruciatingly pale with blonde hair strewn in fine careless disarray all over her head. I knew at once that she had never eaten banana bread in her whole entire life and had, in fact, never even aspired to eat banana bread.

After the greetings, she smiled faintly and said, "We view your house with admiration, though from a distance and through the foliage."

Nick chimed in, "We like the cedar and stone. Did you design it yourselves?"

"No," Tom replied, "we just found it, driving around out here with friends. The real estate people didn't show us anything in this neighborhood. They kept taking us out west. We tried to tell them what we wanted, but . . ."

"Right!" Nick said. "Know what you mean." He opened the car door and placed the banana bread on the seat. "Sorry to be abrupt, we're on our way to the movies. Really would like to see your house sometime."

Daphne moved toward the door on her side of the car, tugging at her halter. "Yes, to be sure," she echoed, sliding into the seat.

"We don't want to keep you," I said. "How about coming up for a drink Sunday? We'd love to show you our house."

"Great," said Nick.

"About four?" I asked. "Sundays are pretty relaxed at our house."

"Four will be fine," he agreed. Daphne blinked and again smiled faintly, and they whisked off as if the Olds were a royal coach.

It was sometime after four when the doorbell rang that Sunday. I hastened downstairs to open the door. I could not have been more surprised if the Ghost of Christmas Past had been standing there. Nick looked relaxed in turtleneck and corduroys. But Daphne was wearing a pale pink dress with a sweetheart neckline and a swishy skirt, high-heeled pink sandals, and a black picture hat with one pink rose at the crown. Her face had been pinkened. The blonde hair had been pulled, a curl at a time, from under the hat, so that dozens of blonde ringlets framed her pink cheeks under the shadow of the brim. I had not seen such a costume since my mother's friends gave tea parties in my hometown years before. Thinking of my own knit shirt and wrap-around, I thought I might just as well have left on my jeans.

Somehow we all made it to the top of the stairs. We introduced Robert and Claire, our children, and stood back to hear our neighbors' comments about our house, which looks out banks of windows right into the treetops, with the Smokies visible on clear days as a distant blue wave. Their remarks were just as favorable as we had anticipated. They began to recite descriptions of the interesting houses they had seen while house-hunting and to explain rather comfortably how they had chosen the Taylor house.

We drifted into the living area to sit down, and I saw for the first time what writers mean when they say "the lady arranged her limbs." Daphne arranged her limbs on the sofa, maintaining her regal posture all the while. I was not dismayed. I was prepared to engage this fine creature in conversation—I was going to rely on an opening I had heard about, when my friend Joan moved into her house on Dellwood next door to the Watermans. Joan, who is herself not your ordinary housewife, had been invited for a cup of tea by Mrs. Waterman, a white-haired person of some rank in their neighborhood. Once they were settled with their tea, Mrs. Waterman had inquired, "And what are your interests, my dear?" This question did not bring up personal matters, religion, or politics—perfect! Warming to the opportunity, Joan had discussed China, British literature, and Texas cooking—and afterward reported favorably on her hostess's sensitivity and intelligence.

But first, of course, we had to offer our guests refreshments. Here, too, I was prepared. I had spent the morning separating a chicken from its skin and bones, mincing the meat, a little celery, a little onion, a few pecans, combining all with mayonnaise thinned with broth, to be slipped by the spoonful inside miniature cream puffs just before serving. So while Tom made the drinks, I prepared the savory puffs. Daphne had asked for a glass of white wine. We felt lucky to have a bottle of Almaden Chablis chilled. In a few moments, Robert and Claire faded away to their own teenage pursuits.

Tom handed the glasses around. I set the tray of chicken salad cream puffs on the coffee table. We were all set, I thought. But, with little shakes of the picture hat, Daphne declined to taste a single puff. She sipped her wine as if it were Listerine. There was nothing to do but get on with conversation, to say, with just the right friendly tone, "And what are your interests?" I had never meant to say *my dear*, having neither rank nor age with which to patronize anyone. I smiled at her and asked, "And what are your interests?"

Daphne drew back, stiffening her face and her spine at the same time. Frostily, she answered, "I did not know I came to be interviewed."

So much for thinking I was prepared. I do not remember anything else that she and I might have said. I do remember that she searched nervously through her purse for a cigarette, awkwardly stuck the thing in her mouth, and proceeded to light the wrong end of it. Nick and Tom were exchanging university chit-chat in animated fashion. Nick had a second drink, ate several chicken salad cream puffs, and pronounced them delicious. Soon he said they really must go, they were expecting guests for dinner. Daphne un-arranged her limbs, reclaimed her upright regal posture, and adjusted her hat ever so slightly. She smiled a brief and uncomfortable smile, a sort of polite grimace, actually, and we escorted them down the stairs.

Once we had closed the door, Tom and I clambered back up the stairs and collapsed in the living room to try to figure out what kind of social event we had just hosted. All I knew was that I had been out-Southern-belled by a Yankee.

***

As time passed, Nick and Daphne eclipsed all other neighbors in newsworthiness. The grapevine had never been better, giving rise to wonderful stories about their tastes and habits. She had worn a mink-trimmed sweater to the supermarket. And she had to call a taxi to get there—she had never learned to drive. She found our symphony less than euphonious. She drank only imported wine (Almaden! Chablis!). She served stuffed grape leaves and paté from New York. She was homesick. She was pregnant.

Late one spring afternoon, I glanced out the window as a taxi pulled up in their driveway. Daphne withdrew from its interior with three or four armloads of groceries, which she set on the front steps. Then the taxi also withdrew—but she tripped around the house and reclined on the hammock in the backyard. I realized she must have locked herself out of the house.

I continued writing—books, legal pads, dictionary, and style manual spread in profusion all over the dining room table. This paper was to be the most insightful and original of my graduate school career; it deserved my concentrated attention. But the April sun soon dropped behind the hills, and I knew that the shadows across their backyard would become uncomfortably cool. It would be at least another hour till Nick would be home . . . and she *was* pregnant.

I pushed my chair back, walked out to the driveway edge of the hill, and yelled down to her, as politely as possible, an invitation for a cup of tea. I was thinking all the while that she probably didn't drink tea made with teabags, which were all I had, even if they were Constant Comment, but that she could at least warm her hands on the cup.

She accepted my invitation with something like eagerness, tripped up the hill, and floated into the armchair at the end of the table. I apologized for the disorder and complained about my labors without mentioning the depth of my insights or the height of my originality. I put the teakettle on, set china cups on the counter—did you think I would use the Melmac?—and whipped out the teabags. She did eventually sip the whole cup away and allowed me to pour a second. She managed to interview me, inquiring about Claire and Robert, whom she saw often as they went up and down the hill to and from the school bus. Presently the Olds pulled up in their driveway; she thanked me for the tea and fluttered down the hill.

In June, Daphne's mother arrived to await the birth of the "little heir or heiress." I was eager to meet her mother. What would the mother of a fairy princess be like? Imperious? Attended by a retinue of servants? Determined to protect the fragile creature who must give birth in the provinces, where mountain midwives might suggest placing a knife under the bed to cut the pain? Wrong again! Her mother greeted me without affectation. She showed no pretensions in hairstyle, clothes, or make-up.

Waiting for a baby's arrival is tiresome. But at last the great moment arrived, along with—not one, but two—babies. I don't know why they didn't know in advance there would be two. The babies were named for Russian princesses but called fondly One and The Other, according to Nick (turtleneck and corduroys). There wasn't a lot of news after they came home from the hospital. No one had achieved the intimacy necessary to be told how much weight they gained or when they slept through the night. Certainly I wasn't going to interview anyone.

They were gone, of course, as soon as travel was feasible, to spend the remainder of the summer on Long Island; but on the day that fall classes were to begin, once again the royal coach appeared in the driveway. I hoped that Daphne had not yielded to what I guessed would be a strong desire to stay in Long Island amid the familiar surroundings of home. In a few days, I was rewarded by the appearance of a twin stroller parked beside the front sidewalk. I sighed with a strange satisfaction that all the princesses were back.

***

Sometime that winter, Daphne called to invite us to dinner. As usual, I seized the opportunity to commit a *faux pas*. Remembering my own efforts to entertain in the presence of infants, I volunteered vigorously to contribute homemade rolls to the dinner. She, no doubt bumfuzzled by this offer, made polite hem-and-haw noises, which I mistook for assent. So it was that we showed up, along with Vaughn and Mary Lou from across the street, at the appointed hour with a panful of homemade rolls. Daphne whisked the pan downstairs into the kitchen while Nick directed us upstairs to the living room, which was suspended over the family room and kitchen below like an architectural dream. With white walls, glass dividers, gray carpet, European antiques, and art objects produced by people who were not relatives, it had the feeling of a museum.

We became subdued, as if we had been invited to a membership party where the price was going to be quite a bit higher than we wanted to pay but where it was going to be impossible to leave without joining. We nibbled at the stuffed grape leaves, wondering, as everyone does upon first eating grape leaves, about the effects on digestion, while we sipped our drinks and listened to stories from Nick (turtleneck and corduroys) about the vagaries of his department at the university.

Daphne moved from living room to kitchen to nursery, a sort of blur of anachronistic domesticity in a silken black sheath with a slit up the side and a very large silver crescent-shaped ornament on her chest that seemed to lack only a label nearby saying "Etruscan, 500 B.C." She invited Mary Lou and me to watch her feeding the babies, propped in infant seats on the bed. I marveled at the daring of a woman who not only dressed in black silk before feeding her babies but also placed their carriers on a satin bedspread—was this what one learned at the Sorbonne? The babies, lovely blonde cherubs, chugalugged their formula and seemed content to burp and coo while we went down to dinner.

Rather hesitantly, we seated ourselves around the glass-topped table. Vaughn and Mary Lou and Tom and I passed around a bracing, reassuring look, the kind with raised eyebrows and a nod. Daphne brought in the first course, oyster soufflé—heavenly. Everything was fine until the main course. She had set our plates before us, each containing what seemed to be a filet and a mound of brown and white rice. The reason we were not sure it was a filet was that it was cooked, sure enough, but not browned. I know now she probably had the first microwave in town, but at the time I was not going to ask her how she had cooked the steaks. She had also set a sauceboat and ladle on the table. Then she returned to the kitchen or checked on the babies or something.

Our eyes fell upon Nick (turtleneck and corduroys). He would know what to do. He picked up the sauceboat and casually ladled the gravy or whatever it was onto the rice. Just as casually we followed his example. As Daphne reappeared, she gasped. The sauce was for the filet! What could we do? It is difficult to remove sauce from rice.

Nick remonstrated with her that the flavors would all blend and mumbled something about how the last time it went on the rice. We said, "Oh, we should have known" and "How silly of me" and similar lame apologies.

Our collective gaffe in no way impaired the excellence of the food. We could only hope that Daphne could detect the sincerity of our compliments and that they would assuage her disappointment over cooking for neighbors who did not recognize a continental dinner while they consumed it. Daphne served my hot rolls along with the French bread. I refused to claim any relation to them, and no one remarked upon their unlikely presence.

In the warmth of alcoholic brotherhood and the heightened pleasure of our taste buds, we began to think of ourselves as witty and worldly, despite all evidence to the contrary in my case. From time to time, Daphne had to respond to a cry from One or The Other. She was quite busy serving the dinner anyway, so she was able to eat only a few bites. We felt sorry for her but reasoned that she would clean her plate in the kitchen after we left. She closed out the meal with strawberries Romanoff—a noteworthy concoction with no taste of Cool Whip—and we enjoyed another few rounds of desultory but elegant conversation.

Vaughn and Mary Lou, Tom and I trudged slowly homeward up the hill, a fine glow pervading our spirits, arising from our new vision of excellence in the culinary arts, a whole new world Daphne had revealed to us, promising endless gustatory delights and perhaps a few human delights as well. The winter stars winked in the black sky, and we were in a spell.

***

All too soon I felt compelled to cash in on the glow. I invited Nick and Daphne to dinner and began to plan a suitable high-church/down-home menu. I also invited a young couple who were in school at the university—Marc and Emily were about Daphne's age. They would give depth to the generation between us and our children. And, as aspiring poets, they would like to hear about the seminar with Anne Sexton that Daphne had attended. I ordered the Smithfield ham, to be boiled, baked, and sliced thin, like proscuitto.

Late on the afternoon of the appointed evening, the phone rang just as I was whipping orange juice into mashed sweet potatoes for my famous Fruity Sweet Potatoes (since renamed Sweet Potatoes L'Orange). It was Daphne, saying that Nick would not be able to come, as one of the babies was not well, and Nick was none too well himself. I removed a place setting from the table and went on with the preparations. At least she had not cancelled out.

The arrivals, the introductions, the cocktails went smoothly. This time Daphne wore ivory silk slacks and sweater to match—elegantly casual. This time we had chilled a bottle of Pouilly Fuissé—William Faulkner's favorite wine, I made sure to say—and Daphne actually swirled it in her wine glass and sipped a few tiny sips, but deigned to partake of the baked brie. Eventually we took our places at the table, and I served the bowls of fresh mushroom soup, simmering with a kiss of nutmeg. The rest of us approached the task with enthusiasm, but Daphne gingerly dipped the liquid with her spoon, just enough to take a taste.

I looked toward Marc and Emily. "Daphne once attended a seminar with Anne Sexton," I advertised, and then turned to her, "We have read her work and talked about it in the poetry workshop."

Marc's face became luminous. He looked eagerly at Daphne and ventured, "We had hoped to invite her for a campus appearance, but our English department has never invited a woman poet."

"Perhaps," she said slowly, "the department finds the unreliable quality of madness a deterrent to literary performance."

"Maybe so," agreed Marc, "but that has not kept them from inviting a few poets whose literary performances were impaired by a commodity as familiar as demon rum—"

"And complained noisily about it," put in Emily, "after the poets were safely back on the plane."

"True enough," said Marc, turning to Daphne, "but what sort of performance did she give in the seminar? What did she say to the young writers there?"

I interrupted to bring on the salads—avocado and grapefruit on watercress. We passed the pepper grinder so that a few flakes could cascade down onto the honey-mustard dressing and prepare our palates for the peppery flavor of watercress. When the grinder reached Daphne, she began twisting the top instead of turning the grinder. She must have realized that no pepper was coming out because her pale fingers twisted the metal top more rapidly. In less time than it takes to tell, the piece fell off, dropping through her fingers, off the table, and into the shag carpet beside her chair.

It was one of those moments suspended in time that usually occurs when you have received news of a death in the family. You are caught up in the news, and you can feel your unschooled response forming somewhere under your breastbone, a response that simply cannot be expressed because all at once there is too much to do. I shot a look of authority around the table and swooped down to recapture the metal piece from the carpet. I reassured Daphne that the grinder had always been unreliable and that I should have bought another years ago. I replaced the top and demonstrated with one precise turn how to grind pepper. Then I gently handed it to her with just the right unperturbed expression on my face.

Meanwhile, back at the table, there was a lot of eye-rolling going on, which remained confined to eye-rolling by the exercise of a level of control that would have made all our mothers proud. The conversation had skipped a beat, and I was unsure whether to resume the rhythm by recalling Marc's question or to pursue a momentary diversion. I was saved from a decision by Emily, who asked Daphne, "Was Sexton's performance notably mad when you saw her?"

"No-no-no," replied Daphne. "She was, after all, occupied with responding to the direction of the professor and the probing of the students. A certain feverish manner occasionally accompanied her comments, but nothing as severe as madness."

Marc narrowed his eyes. "Robert Lowell is credited with encouraging Sexton, yet even he called her work 'confessional.'"

Daphne tightened her lips ever so slightly. She spoke in a low voice. "When one writes from one's interior, one will find the term confessional applied to one's work; and given in addition the religious nature of Sexton's poetry, its correct application is inevitable, do you not agree?"

"It's a pejorative," Emily interjected flatly, "applied often to the work of women by men of influence."

Daphne's eyes widened. She spoke coolly, "Mr. Lowell himself is not unacquainted with debilitating illness. His life has been marked by episodes of violent behavior and consequent treatment, which I would imagine have served to predispose him toward commiseration with Sexton's illness."

"That certainly establishes," said Emily, "that the English department does not discriminate on the basis of madness."

"He did not show me the energy to be crazy when we heard him read," said Claire. "He seemed like any other old man, nice but fumbly."

"I know what you mean," Marc said to Claire. "He was a shadow, frail and thin and gray."

"Yes," I agreed, "and spoke of the Fugitives as contemporary poets! I wanted to jump up and say 'A lot of them are dead. Have you read anything lately?'"

Daphne permitted herself a small smile. "Quite possibly he considers the Fugitives contemporary because they were *his* contemporaries. To continue to project himself as a central figure in American letters, he cannot present himself as passé."

"Well," said Marc, "if I were one of the most important writers in the country, I'm sure I would not easily give up the power of definition of terms in the field of literature."

"You mean we can just ignore fifty years if we want to?" said Claire.

"Sure," said Robert, "the last fifty years don't matter to English teachers, anyway."

Marc and Emily were smiling in amused agreement, and Claire looked pleased. I removed the salad plates—Daphne had barely tasted hers, pepper or no—and brought on the dinner plates with their rosy ham slices, golden mounds of sweet potatoes, and green stalks of fresh broccoli dusted with Parmesan cheese. Tom poured the wine—an Antonelli's Pinot Grigio—and smiled like a patriarch. I passed hot buttermilk biscuits and butter and pointed out Grandmother's blackberry jam in the little crystal jar.

Emily persisted. "Is the interior, then, unworthy of writing about? Is that not what men want women to think—that it is all right to investigate the Confederate dead, and the Union dead, and all the other wars and battles except those that rage within?"

We all looked at Daphne. She inclined her head slightly. "The matter of distinguishing topic from treatment is a further consideration here; but, on the face of it, a writer must view the classification of topics into those that are worthy and those that are unworthy as a constraint not to be borne at all." Emily looked satisfied.

"Yes," I confirmed, "do you know Sexton's poem 'The Touch'? 'For months my hand had been sealed off / in a tin box. Nothing was there but subway railings./' I would never have tried to write a poem about a lover's touch, but she did, and that poem alone is worth the price of the book."

"In paperback, anyway," grinned Tom.

But Daphne was not eating her food. She was stirring it. Just as I had once refrained from looking at her halter top, I now refrained from looking at her plate. What could I say—"Oh, come now, that ham is good" or "Just an eensy bite of potatoes, honey" or "Thousands of people eat biscuits every day"? You see the problem.

By and by I cleared the table. I have never before or since removed a plate so full of rearranged food as Daphne's. Next I served the red-hot apple pie, topped with picture-perfect scoops of vanilla ice cream, with cups of coffee, of course. She didn't eat the pie either, quietly letting the ice cream trickle down through the beautiful red slices held captive by the lattice crust. Everyone else offered lavish compliments.

We trailed into the living room, carrying our cups for one last cupful around the fire. Daphne told amusing anecdotes about Cambridge by way of guidance to Robert, who was applying to Harvard, and inquired about Claire's possible choice of college. Then she said she must go, Nick was really not well, and he would have tended both babies for quite a while now. She swept to the door and wafted away. The winter stars may have winked again, but the spell was broken.

***

They moved back to New York, of course, but not soon, not before the twins grew into toddlers and The Other got lost in the woods. Playing with them in the backyard, Daphne had dashed inside to change One's diaper. Hurrying out again, she had found The Other nowhere to be seen, and the Doberman gone, too. Up and down the street, she called for the errant child and dog, clutching One in her arms. She couldn't guess which direction to take—the five houses were surrounded by woods and hills, you know.

Suddenly three deputies' cars converged on our street, officers talking to Daphne and peering this way and that into the trees. Alarmed, we poured out of our houses. But before the deputies could organize a search, Dr. Masterson strolled out of the woods at the end of the street, carrying the young wanderer. The Doberman, Mary Lou's basset, and the Petersons' German shepherd were romping along in the best of spirits. Dr. Masterson had heard the dogs barking down in the ravine and, upon investigating, had found the little girl sitting on a log swinging her feet while the dogs played around her, like something out of a Black Forest tale.

The Other's cherubic face was flushed with the childish pleasure of taking a walk in the woods. Daphne's face was shining with tear-streaked joy—the joy that is possible only after life-threatening loss of innocence. Reaching out to clasp The Other to her heart, Daphne still held onto One, snuggling both little girls at the same time.

My own mother's heart knew that kind of joy—as a toddler,

Robert had once dashed willfully into the street, and Claire had once lost herself among the aisles in a furniture store. I wanted to hug Daphne, somehow to reassure her about this heart-rending commonality of parenthood, to bond with her, mother to mother. But for once I restrained myself, content merely to witness her joy, to smile silently, and to send good vibes across the unyielding distance and through the obscuring foliage between her life and mine.

***

Shortly after this episode, we heard they were leaving. Nick's new situation was said to be a temporary appointment, but I knew they would not be back. I hated the sight of the moving van in their driveway.

The people who bought the house were coming from California, sold airplanes for a living, had teenage boys who raced dirt bikes, and planned to put in a pool. I pulled out the banana bread recipe and stuck it in the cardholder. But I put it back in the box. I made a batch of my very own chocolate chip cookies—with a touch of orange peel to spark the chocolate—and strolled down the hill to meet the new neighbors, cookies in hand.

We never heard from Nick and Daphne again, but the other night there was a luna moth, pale and fluttery, pirouetting on the glass around the back door.

No Danger to Self or Others

Anne Meek

It was five or six years after Bonnie Baby died before Violet told me. She'd been busy with her career, I'd been busy with mine, and there were no more family reunions where we'd see everybody and keep up with each other; no more gossip about weird cousins or those considered normal in every way. Time—just the turning of the leaves on the wall calendar—has a way of rearranging all the things you took for granted while you were growing up. You didn't realize the calendars would one day come tumbling down like the walls of Jericho, putting an end to homemade-ice-cream-Saturdays and fried-chicken-Sundays, kind of like seedlings in the garden, drying up and blowing away because you forgot to water them. The old people were the ones who had grown up together on the farm, where everybody's work was important to everybody's welfare—the inclusive enterprise called "the family." One by one, without giving much advance notice, they dropped out of sight, and once they were gone, you didn't know how to retrieve or restore their old habits and customs.

So time goes by, nothing you can do about it. The family branches multiply and, for the most part, prosper. The children get educated, get jobs, move away, join other churches or the union or the military or even the country club. And nowadays nobody even knows how to make ice cream in the old hand-crank wooden freezers or how to fry chicken in the old iron skillets. Nobody lives within a day's drive of the home place, so nobody stops by just to visit or catch up on the crop or check on Granny's rheumatiz. Nobody even has the habits of family any more, know what I mean? That sense of duty or obligation or love or common connection—whatever it is—fades at sunset some night and doesn't come back next morning at sun-up. There's no Aunt Bess or Uncle Gene or Grandpa to insist on getting together, no authority to hold us steady in place like an anchor or draw us back home like a giant magnet tugging on our hearts.

All that's left are a few Christmas cards and now and then a birthday phone call. That's how it was that Violet came to visit us during the World's Fair in Knoxville. I had written a note on her Christmas card to invite her to come for the Fair, saying it wasn't too long a drive from Charlotte, and it wouldn't cost her anything to stay with us. So, sure enough, she came that summer, and that's when she brought me up to date about Bonnie Baby—not just her death but her life, or some of it.

When she started on it, it was like turning the pages of one of those old photograph albums Dad used to keep, the first one when he was at the university. Today the old snapshots are falling off the crumbling black pages, some labeled with names, a few with dates and places, most vaguely familiar yet unaccountably strange. It's hard to make anything coherent out of the jumble, I can tell you.

As Violet talked, the pictures in my mind were like that. I could remember the only, absolutely the only, time I had ever seen Bonnie Baby. It was at Aunt Bess's house in Dresden, which is of course not there any more. I mean, we're talking fifty, sixty years. It was next door to the Methodist church, about a block or two from the courthouse where Uncle Rando practiced law and became a judge.

The house was a white frame Victorian, carpenter Gothic really, nothing fancy, but sweet and homey, no turrets or Queen Anne towers, just a wraparound porch on two sides and that curlicue bric-a-brac trim all around. If you went all the way through the kitchen and out on the back porch, you'd see more of the gingerbread trim along the roofline of the house. Then if you went down the back stairs, you'd be in a tiny backyard, with a path across it to the big vegetable garden.

The only time I saw Bonnie Baby must have been one of those fried-chicken-Sundays, when Elma and Mr. Stewart—Aunt Bess's daughter and son-in-law—came home from Nashville, bringing Bonnie Baby and Stewart Jr. to visit their grandparents. I don't know. I was only five years old—it was before Pearl Harbor.

Bonnie Baby must have been twenty at least. She was sitting on the piano stool in the parlor, with her back to the piano, still and quiet. She had on a white eyelet dress, ruching at the shoulders, and a pale blue ribbon around her neck with a little seashell dangling from it. She was so pale she could have disappeared, like a ghost, any minute. Her hair looked like doll's hair, fluffy and blonde, and I saw her twist a lock with her hand and put it in her mouth for a moment. She seemed to look at me from far away. She didn't talk to me . . . or anyone, as far as I can remember.

I know now that she looked ethereal, otherworldly, but then I only knew she wasn't right. I was afraid of her. I held onto my mother's hand.

In Aunt Bess's parlor, you had to look carefully to see anything clearly. The big front window was covered by worn, dark red velvet draperies, complete with filmy glass curtains, too. In front of the draperies stood one of those square Victorian tables with a fringed shawl over it. And on the table stood the usual Victorian lamp with two hand-painted flowery globes, a lamp designed as illuminated art, not as light for reading. Near the piano was the usual curvy Victorian sofa covered with gold-and-red stripes, frayed on the arms, along with the usual curvy Victorian side chairs upholstered in rose red velvet, showing shiny spots of wear all over. The lines of the furniture were blurred by the induced twilight. Any stray ray of light might have revealed dust motes or called forth spirits. The parlor rug was some sort of hand-hooked floral pattern, all the cheer choked out of it by too many footsteps or too many spring-house-cleaning beatings on the clothesline or too many dust motes and spirits. Maybe it was all that worn shabby Victorian darkness surrounding Bonnie Baby's strange pale beauty that frightened me when I was little.

You can see why, listening to Violet telling how Bonnie Baby talked herself out of the asylum, I thought of old family photo albums, images disjointed, pages disintegrating into fragments. Where did these family mysteries come from . . . these cases where no one told the whole story, where all the unpleasant details were simply omitted? In the old days, people typically didn't use certain words—*pregnant* and *cancer* being two of them, if you can believe it. I could see that time's passing wasn't the only cause of my ignorance about Bonnie Baby. Like a giant eraser, a cloak of privacy as deep and dark as Aunt Bess's draperies had fallen across the family secrets.

That was why, I figured, no one had a name for what was wrong with Bonnie Baby—that and the fact that Elma had become a Christian Scientist and would not take Bonnie Baby to any kind of doctor for a long time. Elma simply didn't want to know the name of Bonnie Baby's condition. If she'd had a word for it, she would have had to pronounce it and admit it and do something about it. She preferred her own dream world, and she could always pray about it.

But as Elma and his father grew older, Stewart Jr. confronted them about their own impending mortality. He even said the words "inevitable death"—who would take care of Bonnie Baby then? She had never lived a single day without someone watching out for her, every minute. She had been in school maybe ten days in her whole life. She was never a discipline problem, and she could certainly talk and sing, but she didn't know how to play with the other children, and the three R's seemed to elude her. In the classroom, she only wanted to water the potted plants, and on the playground, she'd collect fallen leaves, pick dandelions and red clover and even the purple blossoms of vetch.

It was clear that Elma and Mr. Stewart had to stop living in a dream world. How could they be sure Bonnie Baby would be properly cared for, without them, for the rest of her life? It was time to make plans. Stewart Jr. had his own family to look after and an important career to manage. He was a big wheel in state government, and some people said he'd be ready to run for governor in a few years. The daily care of an incompetent or retarded sister did not fit into his plans. Besides, with all his lawyer skills and political contacts, he could direct and guide his parents to plan for Bonnie Baby's care.

Somewhere along the way, Elma and Mr. Stewart accepted a solution, Violet explained, even though Elma had to set aside Christian Science for the moment. Little by little, they presented Bonnie Baby to a bevy of doctors, one after the other, and subjected her, time and again, to every sort of physical and psychological examination, until at last the panel of doctors agreed there was no cure. They all agreed that the solution was for Bonnie Baby to be committed to the state asylum for the insane, promptly and permanently.

When this happened, there wasn't any talk about it, in the family tradition of saying nothing about unpleasant realities, especially anything requiring the use of terms like *schizophrenia* or *retardation* or *birth injury*. Saying nothing was the best cover-up possible. And by then Aunt Bess was long gone, as were my dad and their other brother and sister, so the family grapevine was all dried up. And as I've said, we were busy working and raising our kids and making our marks on the world. The fate of Bonnie Baby was not high on our priority lists.

I can only imagine how her parents moved Bonnie Baby into the asylum, bag and baggage. I can only imagine how they prepared her for the move. It probably was harder on Elma than anyone else. She probably went to the asylum every day to see after her daughter, taking care of herself as much as taking care of Bonnie Baby, her first-born, her "beautiful baby."

It was a good thing, all around, I'm sure, that Bonnie Baby was compliant by nature. She probably eased into hospital routines without complaint. The grounds of the asylum were like a city park, actually—beautiful, with hydrangeas, hollyhocks, and roses planted in sunny spots among the wooded borders of tall trees inside the tall iron fence. She helped the asylum gardeners care for the extensive flower beds and the capacious vegetable garden, in the same way she had helped her mother and grandmother in their gardens. She was quiet and sweet; she didn't make trouble. She even learned to make friends, as Stewart Jr. and Violet found out later.

I imagine also that, once her parents had taken their places in Morningside Cemetery back home, Stewart Jr. and his wife Stella would visit Bonnie Baby at the asylum now and then. Maybe they took her on Sunday drives around Nashville. Maybe they even had her out for Sunday dinner at their house when the legislature was not in session, and they had no pressing social obligations. Really, Bonnie Baby just slowly faded off everybody's radar screen.

So, that June when Violet came to the World's Fair, the story she brought with her was astonishing—Bonnie Baby had talked herself out of the asylum. She had not asked Stewart Jr.'s permission, she didn't tell anyone her plans ahead of time, nor did she explain that another person figured into those plans. She simply showed up one day at the desk of the asylum superintendent's secretary and asked for an appointment with Mr. Ingalls. The secretary wanted to know what about, and Bonnie Baby had replied, "My future."

The secretary explained that only the doctors typically made appointments with Mr. Ingalls to discuss treatment options, so maybe she should talk over her future with Dr. Albritton or Dr. Sanchez. Bonnie Baby replied that she had already done that, and now it was time to talk to Mr. Ingalls.

So, Violet said, the secretary made the appointment for the next Tuesday or Wednesday or whatever. Imagine her surprise when Bonnie Baby showed up with Dennis, another resident, whom she proceeded to introduce as her "gentleman friend." Once shown into Mr. Ingalls's office, they explained they wanted to change their place of residence from the hospital to the apartment hotel not far away, just across the boulevard. Bonnie Baby would continue to assist the gardeners with the flower beds, and Dennis would keep on working in the vegetable gardens and the orchards—these provided much of the produce for the hospital kitchen. They explained that neither of them was receiving any treatment that required them to reside at the asylum, and neither of them had any condition making them a danger to self or others.

Bonnie Baby and Dennis were perfectly calm and polite. Mr. Ingalls could only hem and haw and say he would talk with the doctors and with their next of kin. Bonnie Baby and Dennis said they would like to attend that meeting, too. Of course, as soon as Mr. Ingalls called him, Stewart Jr. hurried to the asylum, Violet said. He steered Bonnie Baby to a private spot on the patio and asked her what in the world she could be thinking.

Bonnie Baby drew in a deep breath. "Mother and Father put me here because you told them to. You didn't want me in your house, and there was no other place for me to go. I'm not mad about that. You were right. But I want to live grown up before the Lord calls me to Heaven."

Violet was only repeating what Stewart Jr. had told her, she said, and it might not be exactly word for word, but I'd get the picture.

Anyway, Stewart Jr. said something like, "But we all need someone . . ."

Bonnie Baby had an answer for that. "Dennis will take care of me, and I'll take care of him. We will do our jobs here and see our friends. We can walk back and forth from the Cumberland Hotel—that's where we plan to go . . ."

"But you have doctors and nurses here," Stewart Jr. interrupted.

"For what? I'm not taking shock treatments."

Stewart Jr. started on another tack. "What do you know about this Dennis? Is he, uh, taking advantage of you?"

"Of course not." Bonnie Baby frowned. "We are proper people. He is from a very nice family. We are friends."

Stewart Jr. said he only wanted her to be safe and, then, her blue eyes looking intensely and unflinchingly into his blue eyes, she said, "But I want to be happy, too."

Violet said that got to him, all right. How could he disagree?

She added, "I already talked to Dr. Albritton and Dr. Sanchez. I'm 'no danger to self or others.' Dennis is the same—'no danger to self or others.'"

"Of course . . ." he began, but she interrupted.

"You owe me this, Stewart Jr. You put me in here. You can get me out. You won't be sorry, I promise. I will always be a good girl. . . ."

And she made another point. "At the meeting, I am the one to tell this. Your job is to say *yes* and do the paperwork. Okay?" Stewart Jr. could only say he would see what he could do.

On the appointed day, Stewart Jr. came to the meeting as Bonnie Baby's next of kin, and Dennis's nephew came for him. Violet's understanding was that Stewart Jr. more or less acted as legal counsel for everybody. Bonnie Baby and Dennis explained they did not need to live in the asylum and they wanted to "live grown up" before they died. Stewart Jr. fell in with their plan exactly as Bonnie Baby had asked him to, questioning the doctors and emphasizing that Bonnie Baby and Dennis could continue to work at the asylum and see the doctors as needed. At the same time he took care of the legal issues for Mr. Ingalls and the doctors—nobody questioned how he played both sides, since there was no charge to either. Violet said Stewart Jr. would not have wanted to ruffle anybody's feathers, in case he ran for governor, and Mr. Ingalls would not have wanted to ruffle his, because Stewart was already influential in state government.

Violet didn't say how long it took to iron out all the issues, but eventually Bonnie Baby and Dennis moved a few blocks away from the asylum into adjoining rooms at the old rundown Cumberland Hotel, which had numerous elderly residents paying the rent from social security and welfare checks and eating in a dining room as faded and dated as Aunt Bess's parlor. She did say, laughing a little, that Bonnie Baby repeatedly explained that she and Dennis were certainly not, absolutely not, "sweethearts." They were just good friends who wanted to "live grown up" before the Lord called them to Heaven.

I grinned when Violet said this and raised my eyebrows. Violet shrugged her shoulders and said Aunt Bess would have been proud of Bonnie Baby for saying that, because it reflected her childhood training to become a proper Christian lady from a highly respected family. Whether it was true or not didn't matter. Violet and I understood and agreed about that, even while we were laughing.

Violet went on to say that, when the Angel of Death came for Bonnie Baby a few summers later, her body was of course taken back to Morningside Cemetery to the family plot. Stewart Jr. and Stella brought Dennis with them from Nashville. A few old friends of the family came to the service at First Methodist, and everyone went to the cemetery for the interment. Some time later, Stewart Jr. and Stella had a stone erected, with the words Bonnie Baby on the top line, then a happy cherub in the middle, and her surname, parents' names, and her birth and death dates below. Violet had seen the stone; I hadn't, but I loved the idea of the happy cherub.

After the service, of course, Stewart Jr. and Stella had taken Dennis back to the Cumberland Hotel. No one in the family ever saw him again. But, Violet said, every year for five or six years more, on the date of Bonnie Baby's death, the cemetery caretaker would find a bouquet of wild roses and Queen Anne's lace, sometimes red clover or daisies, laid ever so carefully at the foot of the stone. The flowers were always held together with some sort of ribbon, and there was always a scrap of paper strung on the ribbon, with the words "I love you . . . Dennis."

Josie Higgins

Lu Motley

The hollow had mostly miners' shacks, deserted by the company when coal gave out. The windows were dark like abandoned souls standing on both sides of the hollow. Companion outside toilets bore testament to a vanished way of life. A life which left too many women widowed; too many men broken.

The mines had offered work, though sadly deficient in its humanity. It was taken for granted that those who had been reduced to poverty by the harsh climate and remoteness were inferior to the mine owner, who sat in a house on the hill and played God by controlling the Company Store. He also sublet houses, where the miners lived and returned to after long hours from before sun-up to sundown. This life reduced the miners to survivalists who seldom felt or saw much of anything else.

It was in this climate that Josie Higgins prevailed, with her lively, wild, and vivid imagination. Everyone at Paint Creek School liked Josie. The principal at the school, Miss Owens, was a special friend, who had known from the first day the obstacles the girl faced.

Most of the miners' children wore the same defeated expression of their fathers. But, for some reason, Josie rose above the pain by telling her stories. No one cared if all her characters were familiar. Familiar faces that showed hardship and rejection, except in Josie's stories where people won the battle. The Higgins family, like the others in the hollow, was a large family with nine mouths to feed. Plus, since the men depended on the mines for work, money was scarce.

Miss Owens delighted in Josie's stories, which had a therapeutic effect on the students; when all Josie's characters came to life, another world was created. Thus Miss Owens suggested Josie enter one of her stories when the *Charleston Gazette* down in Charleston, the state capital, offered a fifty-dollar cash prize for the best story from an eighth-grader. The idea that cash would be offered for something that came out of someone's head was amazing.

Mrs. Higgins, simply dressed and rugged-looking from having too many kids and too much hard work, was called to the school by Miss Owens.

"I asked you here to sign the entry form, Ms. Higgins."

"We mountain folks might seem harsh. It comes with the life . . . still a fifty-dollar prize is a lot of money. 'Specially for something that isn't really true. . . . I had to talk to her daddy. He wasn't too sure . . ."

However, she signed the paper and left.

"Funny the difference money makes," Miss Owens mused.

Josie sent in her story about her Uncle Rudy . . . a fascinating fella. Then! Sure thing! Josie won the contest! So Miss Owens had an assembly out on the school ground where students could sit comfortably and eat their brown-bag lunches while they listened to Josie read her winning fifty-dollar story. Josie's dad knew Josie needed something to make her taller so she could be seen, so he built the podium for the occasion. Everyone in that family did their part.

Students were seated on bleachers with their teacher, Mrs. Williams. Josie and both parents were sitting near the podium.

Miss Owens gave Josie a nod. Josie, looking a little scared, stepped up to the podium, cleared her throat and began:

"My Uncle Rudy used to live with us up the holler where the road branches. He's my mom's brother, and he only has one eye because the other was lost in the war. Bad things happened in that war. My uncle found that out when he was shot in the face. Uncle Rudy was sent to the hospital for a long time. Then, they sent him home because he couldn't fight any more with only one eye.

"That's when my uncle came to live with us. We all knew it would be crowded for a while—at least till Uncle Rudy got a job and could find his own place. So right away, Uncle Rudy started looking for work. He got up every morning and walked down to the head of the holler where he would catch a bus to go looking.

"Because times are hard, the mines wouldn't hire a man with just one eye, even if he had gone to war for his country, so Uncle Rudy looked for a job for the longest time. Spring came and then summer, and then it was almost fall."

Josie sighed with a far-away look. "Even though it was crowded with another mouth to feed, and things got pretty bad, Uncle Rudy knew we needed a break, so he took mom and me to the carnival when it came to town. We rode the Ferris wheel and the octopus and the carousel before Rudy's money gave out. Then mom said it was time to go home. I knew she hated to say it because she was having a good time too. Then Uncle Rudy saw someone he thought he knew, so he went over to say, 'Howdy!'

"When Rudy walked over, the man gave him a hug. They laughed, and his friend slapped my uncle on the back. I heard him call Uncle Rudy, 'Sergeant!' They talked for a long time before Uncle Rudy came over and gave my mom some money to take me and get my favorite food—a hot dog! We left Rudy and his friend there talking. My uncle is like that; I mean the only money he has comes from the government because of his one eye. But he still ain't stingy.

"So, later, when Uncle Rudy came to get us, he had a big smile. He wouldn't say why; he just looked happier than I'd seen him in a long time. Then, when Mom asked him what had happened, he said he'd tell us later. Then he smiled as he gave mom a hug.

"The next day, my uncle was gone before I got up. I just figured he'd gone out huntin' for a job as usual. When he came home that night, he had some tickets to the carnival, which he gave to Mom. 'You can now take the whole family,' he told her because that's where he'd gotten a job.

"It was hard to wait till then, but sure enough, that Saturday all us Higgins went walkin' down out of the hollow. As we walked the mile toward the carnival, we were drawn by the smells of popcorn and hot dogs. When we got there, I noticed some signs in front of big tents, and these signs had bright lights of every color with loud music playing. One of those signs read: THE AMAZING RUDY! KNOWS ALL—SEES ALL! COME INSIDE AND MEET THIS GREAT MAGICIAN WHO TELLS YOUR FUTURE!

"Everyone in the family was so excited that they rushed right in and took up a whole row of seats! The suspense was awful as we waited to see what Uncle Rudy was going to do. My Mom chewed on her nails, and my brother's knee began to jerk up and down. Dad just sat there with a disbelieving look on his face.

"Well, let me tell you, we were not disappointed! After about two minutes, a man all dressed in black and wearing an eye patch and a turban with a big white and red feather sticking up in the front walked out on the little stage. It was my uncle! It was Uncle Rudy! I didn't know he could look like that! He was so handsome I had to look twice, and again before I knew it was really him.

"Well, the first thing this man with the eye patch did was to take a tall black hat and hold it up to show that there was nothing in it.

Then, he broke an egg into the hat and took a black and red scarf out of his pocket inside his coat and put it over the hat. Next, he waved a stick over the hat and said a couple of words, which my Dad said sounded like mumbo-jumbo. And do you know something? When the Amazing Rudy pulled the scarf off the hat, a baby chick hopped out peeping. And guess what? He called me up front and gave the chick to me!

"The audience loved that trick! But they liked it even better when a pretty girl in a red and black bathing suit, very high, shiny heels, and a big red feather in her blonde hair walked onto the stage. She turned to the audience and smiled. My dad became more interested as Uncle Rudy pulled out a long, black table and told her to get on it. She did, and the audience yelled and laughed. My uncle began to say some more mumbo-jumbo. (I think it was the same mumbo jumbo he said over the hat before the egg turned into a chicken.)

"And do you know what happened next?"

Several students' heads began to nod yes, before Josie continued. "That girl began to float! She looked like she was asleep in the air when my uncle passed a hoop between her and the table. That scared some people because I could hear some women in the audience gasp. But they must have liked it because they began to applaud.

"After that, Uncle Rudy asked the audience if anyone wanted to have their minds read. Several people stood up, mostly men. Then Uncle Rudy asked them to take their identification out of their pockets and to hold it in their hands. They did that as Uncle Rudy closed his one good eye and told each of those people their age, name, address, and whether they were married or not. When everyone told Rudy he was right, the audience began to clap their hands! And that was the end of Uncle Rudy's show.

"Afterward my Mom and Dad and my brothers and sister just sat there, unable to move. They couldn't believe anyone related to them could be so smart. In about fifteen minutes, Rudy came out from behind the curtain. He had changed clothes and had a box with holes in it; he gave me that box for my little chick. As we walked back home, the whole family began to ask questions. As usual, Uncle Rudy didn't answer right away, but when he did, he had a story to tell.

"Rudy smiled a big smile and told us how glad he was that we all could be there and that we all had liked his show. He then told us about when he was in the war and in the hospital getting well. He had been real depressed about losin' his eye because he didn't know how he could get a job with just one eye. 'I just couldn't get used to havin' just one eye,' he said. 'Then a kind of miracle happened,' Uncle Rudy went on. 'A man who was a magician came to the hospital and offered us veterans lessons in how to do magic, if we wanted to, that is.'

"'Well,' said Uncle Rudy, 'I never dreamed I could use that magic someday to make money. The man who owns the carnival was also in that hospital gettin' over some wounds. I saw him when Josie and her mom and I went to the carnival the other day. It was the first time I'd seen him since I got out of that damn place—the hospital I mean. He asked me if I would like to do some of the magic I'd learned in my own carnival act. I couldn't believe it! Of course I told him I would. The only bad thing is, I have to leave you all and go with them when they leave town, so I thought I better tell you now.'

"We were all sad, and glad too, at Uncle Rudy's good news. That night we had a special meal so all the family could come over and say goodbye properly. My Mom called all my aunts and uncles, and they all brought a dish of something.

"The next week, my Uncle Rudy went on the road with the carnival so he could do his magic. He's still doin' it. Only now he performs for clubs and different groups when the carnival's not in season. Even though I don't see him as much as I used to, I feel like I know my Uncle Rudy a whole lot better now than before he came to live with us."

After Josie finished telling her story, Miss Owens thanked her, gave her the check for fifty dollars, and the photographer from the *Gazette* took her picture. The photographer asked Josie several questions and wrote down what she said. "Tell me Miss Higgins, how do you think of all those things to write?" he asked.

Josie prepared herself before she answered. "Oh it's easy, Sir," she answered. "I just write some of the stories I tell my brothers and sister when I'm watchin' them for my mom."

Later that year, Josie graduated from the one-room school. The very next year, her younger sister, who was in the third grade, was sitting on the playground eating her lunch when Miss Owens came over. The girl was quietly licking the corners of peach fried pie. "How are you today, Mary Louise? Are you liking it here at school?" The principal stopped as she noticed the girl's green eyes light up as she put the last piece of fried pie into her mouth.

"Oh I'm fine, Miss Owens, I'm just fine," Mary Louise smiled, crinkling her eyes; eyes so like Josie's blue eyes. Feeling wistful and missing Josie, Miss Owens continued, "We certainly do miss Josie and her wonderful stories. How's she doing at the new school?"

As though stuck on the same words, Mary Louise responded again: "Fine, Miss Owens, she's doin' real fine." The girl began to brush the pie crumbs into the brown paper bag.

Undeterred, Miss Owens persisted, "How's your Uncle Rudy doing Mary Louise? I really enjoyed hearing about his magic act in Josie's story last year. I thought we might ask him to come to the school some day . . . to do his magic act for us."

Mary Louise whirled around as fast as Miss Owens had ever seen a student move. "Oh, you can't, Miss Owens! Don't you know Josie made up all those stories? We don't have no Uncle Rudy! Lordy . . . Mercy! We don't have any of those people Josie writes about! They all come right out of Josie's head . . . I thought you all knew that!"

With those words, Mary Louise Higgins balled up the brown paper bag and made a long pitch toward the trashcan. Wiping the crumbs off her mouth, she turned and threw her farewell words over her shoulder to Miss Owens. "I guess I'd better get to class, Miss Owens."

Miss Owens stood transfixed, watching where the girl had stood a moment before, not quite knowing what her feelings were. Then, she quickly walked to her office where she closed the door and sat down at her desk trying to dispel a feeling of deep loss.

When Fate Comes Calling

Sandra Ratcliff

He thought we'd gotten away with it. I can't believe he actually thought we had gotten away with it. Every minute of every day I asked myself the same question, "Why?"
"Why had we gotten away with it?"
"Why hadn't anyone been able to find her body?"
"Why hadn't we ever been found out?"
"Why was it that no one could see the guilt written all over my face?"
God knows, I saw it on his face every time I saw him.
"Why her?"
And most importantly to me, "Why had I done it?"
Why in God's name did I ever agree to participate in such a terrible and horrific crime?
Oh, at the time it seemed quite reasonable. In fact, it even made sense to me somehow. All I can say now is that it must have been all the drugs and booze, or at least that's been the best excuse I've been able to come up with in all of these years. Not that it's an excuse, really, but to say that our addiction to the cocaine coupled with our ability to consume large amounts of alcohol on a regular basis had to have been the reason why our plan had seemed to be such a reasonable and even excusable one.

Now, however, as I sit here in the bitter, cold night air on the deck of my lovely, suburban three-bedroom, two-bath home, I question myself over and over again. I replay that terrible night over and over in my head. I'm surprised that as of yet it has not driven me completely mad. As of yet, that is.

"Honey, are you coming to bed?"

My wife brings me back to the moment in time where I physically exist by asking me the same question she asks me at almost precisely the same time she has every night for our entire fifteen years of marriage now. I slowly and cautiously get up from my chipped, worn, faded green Adirondack chair and stumble and sway my way over to where she is standing by the door. I lean in to her and give her a sweet, gentle kiss on the lips and reply to her, "Yes, dear. I'll be up soon. Tell the girls good night for me."

Again, I give her the very same response I've given her night after night. Oh, sometimes it changes up. Sometimes I'm actually able to let go of my guilt earlier in the night, just in time to climb into bed and make love to my wife. Ah, my wife, how I do so love her. Her long blonde locks that fall perfectly around her beautiful, childlike face. How she has been able to put up with me and my drunken, guilt-ridden ways for all these years, I'll never know.

I watch her as she piddles around picking up and straightening the rest of the mess in the kitchen, then turns out the light and heads to bed. She turns to look at me through the sliding-glass door and I blow a kiss to her as she heads up the stairs, once more giving me the same glimpse of adoration, concern, and sadness in her eyes that I see nearly every night. I head back to sit in my chair, stopping along the way to grab another beer from the cooler that I always keep well stocked. I sit back down in my chair, crack off the top to the beer, take a huge gulp, and let it happen. The same thing that happens every night when I allow the memory of her, of that night, and of the events that transpired that night, to enter my mind once again, begging for an answer, begging for an absolution, begging for forgiveness.

It was twenty years ago, less than a week to the day, when it happened. When we rationalized a completely horrid, grotesque, and unbelievably cruel deed and somehow got away with it.

Jimbo, ah, good ol' Jimbo, my best friend since childhood, had swaggered into town for a "surprise visit." Jimbo and I had been friends since we met in military school. It was one of the best military schools around, and our families had both decided to send us there for, as they would put it, "our own good." My father, though loving and caring, was a hard-core military vet. Now he was bound and determined that his only son was going to be, in his words, "a real man who serves and protects his country, proudly," and this was the proper beginning for that, according to him at least. My mother, being the shy, timid woman that she was, quickly agreed with my father and off I went at the tender and impressionable age of twelve.

Jimbo, on the other hand, well his was a different story. His father was (and still is, for that matter) a crazy, no good son of a bitch, who merely wanted to get his children out of his hair.

Jimbo's mother had died of ovarian cancer shortly before he had come to military school. Ever since her death, it seemed Jimbo's old man just wanted nothing to do with his children. He'd sent Jimbo's sister to stay with their grandmother where, luckily enough, she was spoiled, pampered, and ultimately turned into a rich, snooty tramp before finally "settling down" long enough to get married, pop out two (or was it three?), children, then leaving them with their father to become an "actress," as she put it; more like a porn star from what I saw. Jimbo, however, was sent to military school. The two of us met our very first day there and after that, fate took over.

Oh, if only I'd known then what I know now, I would have run. I would have run as hard and as fast as I could have from him the moment he stuck out his long, lanky hand and introduced himself proudly as, "James VanDixon, the third."

Instead of running, however, I stood still. Stood completely still as I, being the four-foot-five-inch runt of a boy that I was at the age of twelve, was overwhelmingly taken and mesmerized by this boy who was only a couple of months older than me, yet he had the makings of a grown man.

Standing nearly a good foot taller than myself, he spoke with eloquence in an already deep, manly voice, and when he spoke, wherever he spoke, he had already had a plan in mind.

You could tell that he had quickly, yet precisely, thought out exactly what he was going to say well before he said it. So, as history would have it, I promptly stuck out my hand, short, stubby fingers and all, and shook his hand to introduce myself.

"I'm Jacob," I said in my still cracking, changing voice that now made me feel only two feet tall. Still, I stuck out my chest, stood up straight (to try to measure up), cleared my throat, and said my name once more, "Jacob Andrew Stuart. Glad to meet you."

From that day on, the two of us were practically joined at the hip. We did nearly everything together; skipping classes, trying weed for the first time, getting drunk, getting high, and getting laid (all in the same night most times, I might add). Yep, Jimbo and I were two peas in a pod, or better put, two urinals in the same john. We were the baddest of the bad-asses that existed in our small, yet prominent, hometown in Colorado. Both of our families were filthy rich and we wanted for nothing. However, when I turned sixteen, my father, being the well-raised and determined man that he was, put me to work when I came home for the summer. I tried to protest, pleading and begging with my father to just let me be a teenager like most of my other friends who already had cars of their own, thanks to the generosity of their parents. My father, on the other hand, was quick to explain to me that having a car was something that came with responsibility, and had to be earned and paid for. Therefore, he sent me off to work at the local convenience store, making a measly $2.25 an hour. I reluctantly went to work five nights a week, having only the weekends off to go party with my friends. However, that was enough time for me to get into plenty of trouble. Not with my parents or anything, but with myself, my conscience. It was during this summer when I got my first taste of cocaine, heroin, and acid.

How I even remember that summer still amazes me, because I spent most of it completely strung out.

I do, no less, remember it, and I remember that it was the summer, as well, that I got my first glimpse at what Jimbo, my pal, my buddy, my best friend, was really going to become—a con man and a thief, among many other things. One night, as a group of us rich, rotten teenage boys sat around getting higher than kites and partied around a bonfire in front of an old abandoned cabin one of the other boys had found and turned into party central, Jimbo pulled me aside and quickly, yet perfectly, described to me the plan that he had been working on. The plan to get a good $5,000.00 from the convenience store where I worked. He described to me everything we would do, step by step, all the way down to the exact day and time that we would pull off this fantastic plan of his. I wanted to protest, wanted to say "No, absolutely not." But you have to understand something about Jimbo; by now, even at the age of sixteen, he stood just over six feet tall with many handsome features, a perfect, nearly hairless body-builder physique, and hip vocabulary. Well, lets just say that in the four years I had known him, Jimbo had nearly perfected his vocabulary by reading dictionaries and thesauruses nightly by the dim light of a flashlight. Not to mention, he was persuasive, very persuasive. He could sell the Golden Gate Bridge to a man living in the middle of a desert and convince him that the water to go under it would arrive shortly after his bridge arrived, shipped to him via UPS, of course. I shook my head in shocked agreement with every detail that spilled from his mouth. What did I know, still shorter than him by a good foot (although it seemed like two), braces, and although what I lacked in height on Jimbo, I easily made up for in massive amounts of body hair, Jimbo had always somehow seemed much more mature and wise than me. And so it began, our days of thieving and conning our way throughout Colorado. Shortly after we graduated from military school, my father promptly helped me enlist in the army and for the first time in six-and-a-half years, Jimbo and I were not together. He stayed behind in Colorado to continue his highly successful career as a con man (though he had slacked off quite a bit ever since he'd met his girlfriend of two months, Stacey), and I shipped off to go to boot camp, and shortly after I was stationed at an army base in Southeastern Virginia. Six years passed as I served my time in the army and settled quite comfortably in a spacious two bedroom apartment with a roommate, just across the water from the base where I was stationed. I missed Colorado, but I loved the beaches in Virginia Beach, and I spent nearly every weekend there, surfing all day and partying all night.

There certainly wasn't a shortage of women, either. I had my pick of women, especially since I had finally grown into a man, and thanks to my three years in the army, I had learned to love the discipline of physical fitness and weight training, all of which was now paying off.

When I first got to Virginia, Jimbo and I would call each other all the time. At first it was almost nightly, then it became weekly, but before too long the phone calls became shorter and shorter and few and far between. It appeared that we were quickly growing apart and each time I talked to him, I realized that he and I had less and less in common all the time.

A good year had gone by since I'd last spoken to Jimbo, and my life seemed to be going fine; perfect, in fact, when I look back now in hindsight of all that had taken place. Then, one day out of the clear blue, there was a knock on the door of my apartment, at six o'clock in the morning of all times. I threw on a pair of jeans that were crumpled up on the floor next to the bed and, hung over, I stumbled my way to the door. I instantly felt like that twelve-year-old boy again when there before me stood a taller, even more handsome than ever, James Leroy VanDixon, the third. I swallowed my jealousy, puffed out my hairy, ape-like chest, wiped the shocked expression from my face; I cleared my throat and managed a simple, "Hey, man. It's great to see you."

In a now booming, commercial-like voice, Jimbo replied back mockingly, "Great to see you? Come here man," and with that, he gave me a great big crushing hug.

I invited him in, quickly apologizing for the mess in my apartment from the guests I had had over the night before. Jimbo walked to the fridge, opened the door, and rummaged through it until he found two unopened bottles of beer. He opened them both and handed one to me.

I quickly explained that I wanted to be straight when I went to the gym in an hour, and then sat the beer he had just handed me onto my already overflowing coffee table. However, still the convincing Jimbo, he persuaded me to have the beer anyway and instead of hitting the gym as I usually did every Saturday morning, we ended up spending the day drinking and catching up. After spending almost the whole day at my apartment, sitting on my couch, drinking an entire twelve pack, we decided to go out and hit the bars all night. Now, here is where destiny stepped in, and after this night, everything in my life would be changed forever.

"So, man. Can I crash at your place tonight," Jimbo asked, as the taxi cab drove both of our drunk asses home.

"Sure man, but only for tonight. My roommate will be back in town tomorrow." I explained.

"That's cool, man. I can get a hotel room tomorrow until I find an apartment or something," Jimbo conceded.

My head whipped around, instantly making me want to throw up all over the backseat of the taxi cab, and I belted out in utter shock, "An apartment? Exactly how long are you planning to stick around for?"

Jimbo gave me an amused but confused look and simply answered, "For good."

I woke the next morning with a splitting headache and a more-than-queasy stomach to find no Jimbo. I quickly tried to convince myself that it had all been just a bad dream, but the current state of my head and stomach immediately contradicted that idea. I somehow managed to shower and nurse a very large cup of coffee, all after popping a few aspirin, of course. It wasn't until 12:30 in the afternoon that Jimbo showed back up at my door, all bright eyed and bushy tailed, ready to go again, as I still lounged around in a clean pair of boxers and an old raggedy sweatshirt watching some chick-flick on Lifetime. Jimbo swaggered through the door, his arms filled to the brim, like Santa bringing my Christmas gifts, only he forgot to use the chimney. I quickly jumped up to help him unload all of the bags and both twenty-four packs of beer he had come in with.

"Man, you don't stop do you?" I asked him, while still feeling the effects from the night before.

"No, man. Never stop. You stop for too long and you die," Jimbo reasoned, as he began to unload the bags he'd brought in. Out of one of them he pulled a foot long sub from Subway, "Just the way you like it, man," he proclaimed proudly as he handed it to me, along with yet another beer he had already cracked open for me. As Jimbo and I sat in my living room eating our Subway subs and watching yet another sappy movie on TV, he proceeded to explain to me the reason why he had decided to move here where I was, or rather the reason according to him. Still being the naive person that I was, I believed all that he told me, from the part where he explained how a so-called friend of his had swindled him in a business deal causing him to lose nearly $500,000.00 of his father's money, which he had invested into the business, to the so-called friend proceeding to steal his girlfriend, Stacey, right out from under his nose, to the part where he had decided to stop using drugs, get clean, and start a new life on the right track once and for all.

I believed him, bought it all, hook, line, and sinker. I even told him I was proud of him as we sat there throwing back a few more beers and munching on a bag of pretzels.

"So, man, what's the plan for tonight?" Jimbo asked.

By then it was nearly six o'clock in the evening and with his question I suddenly remembered, "Oh, man. I'm supposed to meet up with this chick tonight." I frantically began searching my room for any articles of clothing I could find that even resembled being clean. I showered once more, gargled with mouthwash, and called the girl. Tara was her name and when she answered the phone, she sounded just like an angel, much like she looked. We had made plans to meet at a bar near her house to hang out a while, and she seemed pleased to hear that I was bringing along my oldest, bestest buddy, Jimbo. She, too, had a friend who could use some company, she explained. Jimbo and I arrived twenty minutes late. I had gotten lost on the way and had driven past the place twice, as I later found out when I stopped to ask for directions at the convenience store that happened to be right across the street from the place.

I thought for sure that Tara and her friend would be gone, but as fate would have it, they were still there, posed just right on two bar stools in front of one of TVs in the bar, watching a football game. I remember walking up behind her and asking her, "Who's winning?"

Then she turned around and without hesitation, she gave me a hug. She introduced her friend, Michelle, to both Jimbo and me, and the rest of the night went well. Exceptionally well, in fact. The four of us hung out at the bar for a few hours talking, drinking, and laughing—actually, Jimbo did most of the talking; I was more like a sidekick. I wasn't sure at that moment, but I remembered debating, was I Robin for Batman or was I Donkey for Shrek? Of course with all of the hair that covered my body, I probably more closely resembled the latter of the two.

    Later in the night, we all went back to Tara's house, which was set about a mile off the main road just across the North Carolina line. She owned a huge six-bedroom, four-bath house that she and her ex-husband had bought together. Tara was about forty-five-years old, but she didn't look a day over twenty-one. I remember thinking many times as I looked at her that her ex must have been crazy to have divorced such a sexy woman, but Tara quickly explained to us that he had left her for some twenty-nine-year-old stripper. Tara had blonde hair, cut short, which made her look quite sophisticated; she had one of the most breathtaking smiles I had ever seen; and she loved to workout, which accounted for her flawless physique, despite having two sons who were away at college. But the thing I remember most about her, the thing that to this day still haunts me, were her eyes. Those beautiful, piercing blue eyes that seemed to dance every time she laughed. I'd never met anyone who had loved and embraced life as much as Tara did, despite all of the rotten things that had happened to her in her life. Things such as her husband becoming a drunk, mentally abusing her and using her long after their divorce; several other men had also treated her badly, not to mention the people who had used her only for her money. Still, she embraced life, loved it; she couldn't wait to wake up each new day to see what that new day would bring, at least that's how she explained it. She truly inspired me, a young man of barely twenty-five; meeting someone as happy and as full of life as she was, was truly inspirational for me, and she quickly became someone who I knew that I wanted to be around more often, just so that I could be in the presence of such a happy and positive person. Knowing this, I can't help but to admit that I could never understand just why Jimbo had to pick her of all people, to do what we did to her.

    That night after we went back to her house, the four of us continued to drink, laugh, and we even shared a joint, and before I knew it, Jimbo was practically being dragged from the living room and up the stairs by Tara's somewhat overweight friend, Michelle. He put up a small struggle, but soon gave in; after all, he was going to get laid. Tara and I sat on the couch for a few more hours talking. I loved talking to her; she was obviously an intelligent woman and had successfully started and run her own business. After a few more drinks, the two of us walked up to her bedroom, where we spent the rest of the night having some of the best sex I can remember, even to this day. I'd never tell my wife that, though. The next morning (afternoon actually), Jimbo and I headed back to my apartment. On the drive back, Jimbo proposed yet another deal to me.

"Hey, man, remember I said I needed to find a place to stay?"

Cautiously, I replied, "Yeah, I remember. Did you find a place, yet?"

"Well, no, not exactly," he started, then paused. I remember glancing over at him and I could see the wheels turning in his head.

"So . . . ?" I asked.

"So, I wondered, since your friend, Tara, has that big, old house with no children staying at home, and she's there all alone. . . ." Again he paused. I think that he recognized that this time his persuasiveness might be a bit harder, since I wasn't under the influence of some type of illegal substance. "No, man! Absolutely not. No way," I quickly protested.

"C'mon, man, it's only for a little while. Only until I can find a place of my own. Three months tops. I'll even pay her."

I knew it was a bad idea. I knew it in my head, in my heart, and in my gut. Yet somehow, once again, he managed to persuade me, and before I knew it, I was picking up the phone and dialing her number. Tara hesitantly said yes; that was Tara's one downfall. Even though she had been taken advantage of many, many times in her life, she still lacked the ability to say no.

In fact, it was this very same weakness that would ultimately make her our victim later on.

With in a week, Jimbo was living comfortably in Tara's guest bedroom. Things went fine over the next month. I saw Tara almost every night and the three of us (sometimes four of us) hung out drinking and having a great time. Jimbo, however, quickly gained her trust, which surprised me, since I knew that Tara had been burned enough times in her life that she had no reason to trust anyone, least of all Jimbo. Yet not only did she trust him enough to let him live with her, she confided in him, told him all about her life, her past, her children; she showed him pictures and home movies of her family. Most importantly though, she made the grave mistake of telling him just how much money she really had.

That was it; with that admission, she had given Jimbo the perfect steppingstone to derive his perfectly thought-out plan: to take all of her money and kill her. I knew nothing of this plan until that night, that fateful, dreadful, horrific night when it all took place. It was a Friday night, a dreary, rainy Friday night, when Jimbo suggested that the three of us take a drive back to my place. Tara offered to drive, but Jimbo had already given her a few drinks, one of them laced with Rohypnol (the date-rape drug), which quickly took effect only minutes after we started our journey—our journey to hell, that is. It was when she passed out and I began to get worried about her that Jimbo proceeded to explain his plan to me. Earlier that day, he had somehow managed to get hold of Tara's bank account information and had cleaned out both her savings and checking accounts, transferring all of the money, about $750,000.00 to a phony bank account he'd created using her computer. He'd had a friend help him out with that to make it look like she had simply made a sizable contribution to a charity. He had then managed to perfect her handwriting and had handwritten a suicide note which he had already placed haphazardly beside her bed. Now, the plan was to kill her and dispose of her body so that no one would ever find it, and no one would ever know the truth.

"It's perfect. Foolproof." He boasted while laughing. I remember I began to hyperventilate, and Jimbo made me pull over the car. I got out quickly and ran to an open field and proceeded to puke my guts out. There was no way in hell I was going to go through with this. No way, and when I got finished chucking all of my cookies, I fully intended to tell him this. When I got back to the car, Jimbo handed me a beer and two little funny shaped pills.

"Here . . ." he said, ". . . take these, they'll calm your nerves."

I remember asking what they were, and he produced from his pants pocket a prescription bottle that read "Valium" and had his name on it. Not even taking the time to second-guess my good friend, I took them. Good one, Jimbo had given me some real good shit and it only took minutes for me to be flying high on ecstasy, ready for anything. Since I was half out of it, Jimbo took over the drive. He had already found a little abandoned house, miles off of the main road only minutes from Tara's house. Once we arrived at the "house of Satan," as I thought of it since, we proceeded to carry Tara's limp body into the house, placing her on an old, dirty mattress that was lying in the middle of one of the rooms. Jimbo ordered me to stay with her while he went to fetch something from the car. Had I been lucid enough to do the right thing, I would have pulled my cell phone from my pocket and called the cops myself, but being so fucked up on the drugs, I simply lay down beside her sleeping body and watched her as she slept her last peaceful sleep. I remember I ran my fingers across her face, then across her perfect lips, tracing them with one finger; then I ran one finger down her neck toward her blouse until it reached her breasts. I took my finger and made a continuous circle over and over again around one of her nipples until Jimbo barged back into the room out of breath with his arms once again full, only this time he had rope, duct tape, latex gloves, and hairnets.

"Here, put these on, man." Jimbo ordered tossing the items at me. "Hurry up man, she's gonna start coming around soon." It was all such a blur to me that night, yet as I sit here remembering it now, it all comes in as clear as a bell. We removed all of her clothes, tied her feet and hands with rope, Jimbo stuck a cloth in her mouth and secured it with the duct tape. Shortly after we had finished tying her up, she came to with the most horrific and terrified look on her face. Yet she didn't attempt to scream, didn't attempt to struggle, not even a plea for her life. By now, Jimbo and I had downed an entire bottle of tequila, again to calm my nerves and his this time.

I remember simply seeing the look of terror on her face and one simple tear running down the side of her face. Jimbo was the first to rape her. I remember thinking wasn't it enough we were going to kill her, did we have to rape her, too? He raped her a total of four times over the course of the night, or at least that's how many times I counted. In between his third and fourth time with her I had my turn with her and it was the most unimaginable kind of sickness that I had ever experienced in my entire life. I passed out after Jimbo's fourth time raping her. Jimbo woke me up somewhere around four in the morning.

"C'mon, man. We have to get rid of her body." He said this calmly and matter of factly, like it was simply some unfinished project we needed to complete for school or else we'd be grounded.

Though I was still half drunk, I think the drugs he'd given me had worn off. I looked over at the mattress and saw her beautiful, naked body laid spread eagled now, ropes no longer binding her hands and feet, duct tape no longer covering her perfectly formed lips, breath no longer coming from her—but those eyes. Her piercing, beautiful blue eyes were still wide open looking straight up at the ceiling, never to dance again with her laughter. This, I remember, broke me, broke my heart, my soul, broke my very existence as I had ever known it before, and it haunts me to this very day. I helped Jimbo carry her body to the car where we gently placed her still-naked, lifeless body in the trunk. I sat motionless, stunned and forever changed, as Jimbo drove deeper into the woods for about a half an hour. He picked a spot, and I remember he said, "That looks like a good place." He pointed as he parked the car and then began digging a shallow grave in this so-called "good place," while I watched in absolute disbelief and horror.

When he was finished, I watched as he dragged her battered and bruised body over to the shallow grave and laid her peacefully in the place where she would rest forever. Tears streamed down my face as we covered her body with dirt, and again I saw her blue eyes, only this time her eyes were staring straight through me, as her face was the last part of her I covered with dirt before I finally realized what was really going on here. I dropped my shovel and fell to my knees and with what little strength I had left in me, I cried over her dirt-covered body like a little baby. Jimbo finished the job alone, he discarded of all of the evidence, and not a word was spoken as he drove us slowly back to my apartment. I remember he dropped me off so that I could "sleep off the booze," as he so eloquently put it, and he took my car, vacuumed it out, washed it, and left it parked in the parking lot of my apartment complex with the keys still inside and a note thanking me. He thanked me and asked me to never, ever tell a soul about our heinous crime.

After that night, I never saw him again, and other than receiving an overly stuffed letter-sized envelope which contained nearly $25,000.00, I never heard from him again either, and I never wanted to. I was tempted to keep that money since it was his fault that my life was now going to be forever changed, but when I remembered that Tara had given her life for that money, I quickly took it to the nearby Children's Hospital and gave it all to them. Still, I know, I just know that he thought we had gotten away with it. I know him, the ever-confident, suave, convincing man that he is, that he had always been, I know he thought that for all these years we'd gotten away with it . . . but we hadn't.

You see, every year on the anniversary of her death, Tara would come to me, not in a dream, not in some sort of premonition; she'd come to me to remind me, and in the most angelic voice that anyone would ever wanna hear yet a voice that chilled me to the bones, she would deliver the very same message that she had every time she had come.

"Jacob, you haven't gotten away with it. Your day is coming. Your day and his is coming."

Then, she would go just as mysteriously as she appeared; she'd vanish and leave me to face this terrifying message that she always had for me, year after year. This year was going to be different though, somehow I knew it, I felt it. This year was going to be different, and it was.

Friday, November 20 started out as normal as any other day. My wife and I saw the kids off to school, I kissed her goodbye, told I loved her, and climbed into my black Escalade and headed to work. On my way, however, something caught my eye, and I slammed on my brakes and stopped in the middle of traffic. It was a broadcast of the morning news playing on a big-screen plasma television in the front window of a department store. I jumped out of my truck, leaving it sitting idle in the middle of traffic, and ran toward the department store window. There, before my eyes, was footage of none other than my old pal, Jimbo, lying dead and mangled on the sidewalk. He had taken a twenty-story leap from the balcony of his million-dollar condo after filing bankruptcy on his once multimillion-dollar business "that he had built from the ground up with his own two hands," as the news anchor put it. "Yeah, right . . ." I thought, ". . . from the ground up with his own two hands. More like from Tara's ground up with her two hands."

Turns out that he was being investigated by the FBI for tax evasion as well. I stood there stunned and shocked, yet happy to see the world rid of such a lying, manipulative, filthy, rotten scoundrel such as James Leroy VanDixon, the third. Still, at the same time, I was horrified. Did this mean that my time had come, too? I never meant for any of this to happen, never meant for things to turn out like they did. I never, ever thought that Tara deserved what we did to her. No one ever knew it, but I went to her memorial service.

Almost a year after her "disappearance," I went to the service that her family had for her to help them finally bring some kind of closure to their sudden and mysterious loss, no doubt.

I watched as what seemed to be hundreds of people stood around crying, consoling one another; many were simply inconsolable. I watched as her two sons each placed one white rose on an empty casket. I watched as even her good-for-nothing exhusband laid his wedding band and a white rose on the casket then fell to his knees, only to be picked up and carried away by several other men. It broke my heart to watch the whole thing. Since then, I'd never gone back to that cemetery where they buried the empty casket and called it her final resting place, but today, at this very moment of realization, something or someone, rather, pulled me back into my truck and headed me straight to that cemetery, straight to that plot. So there I was kneeling in front of the headstone that read, "Tara Ann Moore, Loving Mother, Daughter, Sister, Wife, and Friend," and standing guard at the top of the headstone was one simple and appropriate beautiful angel.

I ran my fingers across her name much the same way that I had run them over her sweet lips that last time. It was then and there that I broke down. I screamed, begged and pleaded for forgiveness from both God and Tara for what I had done. When I finally pulled myself together and turned around to head back to my truck, there she stood. Still just as beautiful as ever, she stretched out her arms and gently spoke to me.

"Jacob, come," she said simply. "Come with me now."

"No!" I protested. "I'm not ready to go. I'm so very sorry for what I did to you. So very sorry. What can I do to make it right? Just tell me and I'll do it; I swear, I'll do it."

I begged and pleaded once more before I dropped to my knees in front of her and buried my head in my hands. She reached down and with one finger, she pulled my chin up so that my eyes met her still bright and beautiful blue eyes. She smiled gently and once again those eyes danced, just as I remembered.

"Jacob, I'm afraid your time also has come, but before I take you with me, there are a few things that you must do."

"Anything," I whispered to her. "I'll do anything."

She shook her head and smiled at me once more, "Then come with me," she said, and she wrapped me in her arms. Next thing I knew I was standing in front of a phone booth on a street that seemed vaguely familiar to me. It took a few minutes, but then, out of nowhere, it dawned on me—this was the road that led to the place where Tara's body was buried twenty years ago. I was alone, for now, and instinctively, I picked up the phone and dialed a number I'd never even heard of in my life. A woman picked up on the other end and said simply, "Moore residence." I took a deep breath. "Yes, could I speak with Mr. Moore, please?" I asked the woman, who spoke with a strong Spanish accent.

"May I ask who's calling?" she inquired.

"No, just tell Mr. Moore that this is an extremely important phone call," I explained to her in a calm and even tone. I could hear the phone being put down and then shuffled around, then I heard a new voice speak to me on the other end.

"This is Mr. Moore. Can I help you?"

"Yes, sir. You don't know me, but well . . ." I paused for a moment wishing that I didn't have to do this, wishing that I could turn back time and undo all that had been done. I began again.

"Listen, I have some specific directions to give to you. Please write these down, sir."

Surprisingly enough, the man on the other end didn't even protest; in fact, he sounded somewhat shocked and breathless as he simply replied, "Ok."

I then proceeded to give him the exact directions to the place where Tara's body could be found. I then told him that I would be waiting there for him and to bring his brother and the police along with him. After I hung up the phone and looked up again, I saw Tara. She told me that I had one last thing to do, and without hesitation I picked up the phone once more and called my wife. She asked me what was wrong. I simply told her to remember that I love her and the girls with all of my heart. Then I said goodbye and quickly hung up the phone before she could ask me any questions or beg me to come home, because I knew that that was no longer a possibility. I stepped back out of the phone booth, a now completely broken forty-five-year-old man, and with tears now coming uncontrollably, I walked right back into Tara's arms, which were already outstretched and waiting for me.

What seemed like only a few seconds later, we were standing at the very site where I had last seen Tara's beautiful, mortal body resting. It was now beginning to turn dusk, and in the distance I could hear sirens headed in my direction. Tara looked at me for the very last time. She spoke softly and gently, sounding almost as if she were singing to me as she said, "Jacob Stuart, I have long since forgiven you for what was done to me. God forgives you, too. He heard the prayers that you prayed every night since that night and you are forgiven." With that, she was gone, and I could hear the tires of the police cars screech to a halt behind me. I dropped slowly to my knees and put my hands on top of my head before any of them had a chance to get out and tell me to do so. A couple of cops put me on the ground face down, they handcuffed my hands behind my back and then they stood me back up again. As they walked me to one of the cars, I caught a glimpse of a young, handsome man with Tara's same blue eyes. He turned and looked at me, just before he walked up to me. We both stood there for a moment, just taking each other in. I could not take my eyes off of his, they were the very same eyes. We spoke no words to each other, and he began to walk away; as he did, though, I stopped him and asked him why it was that he had not questioned me when I called him to tell him where to find me and his mother's body. He looked at me with a puzzled expression on his face and said simply, "Sir, I don't know who you are, but it was not you I spoke to on the phone. It was my mother."

They put me in the back of the police car. I sat there for a long time as, outside, detectives and police officers collected Tara's remains and worked on papers. Some even stood around drinking hot coffee and laughing at each other's conversations.

As I sat in the back of the car alone, watching as the last bit of the day's sun disappeared on the horizon, I felt the most excruciating pain shoot up my left arm and into my chest.

It felt like Dumbo himself had landed smack in the middle of my chest. I tried to catch my breath, but it wouldn't come. I tried and tried again, but it was hopeless. The pain in my chest was now unbearable, and I knew then that today, November 20, as I sat alone in the back of that police car, less than twenty feet away from where her body had lain for twenty years—my time had come.

Needin' Mista Sun

Lynn Veach Sadler

My friend, Sheriff Abner Winstead, was worried. He'd heard about drum talk but never in Duplin County. I tried to set his mind at ease. At our place in Hallsville, on the Northeast Cape Fear, drums were regular treats every holiday, and July 4 was coming. The slaves pass drumming down, father to son, a birthright going all the way back not just to the West Indies, where most of our people were from, but to Africa. Their drums and dancing carry their history right along with them. How extraordinary that they could be so violently displaced and still maintain such ties. Abner was not easily pacified, insisted they use drums to pass messages about uprisings, like the one in Stono, South Carolina, that saw thirty Whites killed.

He has fifteen years on me, has accepted his lot, was always pushing me to settle in. "Sherry's not a man's drink, Sam Wesley. To fit in, drink whiskey—and pretend to like it! And throw in cigars for good measure. These your boy Moses makes are as good as any from the West Indies, though you'll just say he proves our slaves capable of being educated. But Moses is not your average . . ." He was right about that.

I felt *buried alive* in the midst of ignorance and downright meanness. I'd finished my medical degree two long years before, had been planted here by Papa to run Freedom Hall Plantation, between Warsaw and Kenansville. I'd taken up art to pass the time, but nothing worked. I was as weary of painting loblollies, acorns, and fake Roman columns as of entering wearisome figures in a ledger. "One tooth extraction for Angus McKennon paid with one pound butter." The most exciting case I ever got was a breech birth—a *calf's!* I hadn't wanted to go to medical school, following Papa's footsteps, but I quickly became entranced. It was so exciting at Harvard. The professors, the research, the feeling that we might be able to help people. Fighting cholera epidemics in

India, East Africa, most of Asia. Another one's just broken out in Europe. What if I went *there?* Too many responsibilities here. Freedom Hall and its people. My sister and niece.

I couldn't fool Abner. "What's happened to stir you up?" He was right. I'd seen *her.* Dancing. In clinging white with an irregular hem. *Amaryllis.* What was Papa thinking when he named her? About that passage he was always quoting from Milton's "Lycidas"? Why would she appear *now?* Why hadn't she come straight to me? She never tried to write me at Harvard. I'd taught her reading and writing.

Amaryllis confronted me after the guests had fled the tea party that afternoon. "Was I just an experiment, Sam Wesley? No! I'll always believe you loved me, but, like every good White man, you were so terribly naive. Things don't come right because a good person wills it. My mama tried to tell me, but I wouldn't listen. I thought you could change the world because you were so good. Oh, why didn't you leave me alone? I curse you by the gods of Mother Africa, by the God you claim as Christian. Your meddling has unleashed the swarm!" She believed I ruined her—but not because I couldn't claim her except in her bit of a back room late at night. "If you'd left me alone, I would have had a life of some kind. With a simple man who didn't know he should change the world. Moses believes he's got to help me do whatever I must. And when it's all over, Sam Wesley, you'll be sorry—but you won't be any different." What did she mean?

Moses' son Ho and my niece Mary Tee, who had been brought up together, got in a tiff over whose turn it was to jump rope. She hit him. He was naturally indignant. I didn't think about his words at the time, but Retrospect is a more diligent taskmaster. I put it down to his never having been treated like a slave. "Looks here, White girl, you ain't hittin' me agin. When we jines Ole Nat, I's feedin' you to his big ole pet rat what lives in this here cave and sit on Mistah Nat shoulder...."

I did question him: "What did you say, Ho? And what was that about gnats and a rat earlier? Were you threatening my niece?"

Ho was as agile-tongued as Moses. "No, Suh, Ho jist fannin' dem gnats outen Miss Mary Tee's eyes so she kin jump rope mo better. Jist promisin' she don't hav to be 'fraid of dem rats wid Ho around. You know how scairt she be ov Mister Rat."

I had to show off again, if only before a young slave. "I certainly do, and she's right to be so. Filthy beasts. They cause plague. You want to catch the plague, boy?"

Abner warned me. "Now, Sam, I don't hold with whippin' Negroes either, but that boy's askin' for a knot upside his head. Too big for his britches, that one."

But I knew that such daily human messes rot a man's soul. "Why can't life be more like it was at Harvard? To learn and learn and learn. My professors talked about vaccines for smallpox, nitrous oxide—'laughing gas'—as an anesthetic. Now we've discovered chloroform, are dissecting cadavers, and laughing at phrenology! Thermometers, stethoscopes, iodine for goiter, hemophilia . . . I'd like to perform tracheotomies, trace vertebrate cells to divisions of eggs and sperms, write something like William Horner's grand anatomical textbook. It came out the same time as that dreadful *Analysis of the Phenomena of the Human Mind*. How could the author claim our minds are nothing more than machines? What if I could prove he's wrong right here with the Negroes?"

Genevra lit into me something fierce when she got wind of Ho and Mary Tee's set-to. Her old lecture about the dangers of "coddling" the Negroes. "You can't even say it, can you? *Slaves*. That's what they are. *Our* slaves. You were bad enough before you went off to Massachusetts, and now you're impossible. Listen to me, Little Brother. This place is half mine, and I won't let you run it into the ground with your fancy liberal notions. That William Lloyd Garrison and his hellacious *Liberator* are bad enough. He's got the Quakers and the Abolitionists around here twaddling of 'freedom.' I heard it all when I was away at that Yankee finishing school. If they just wouldn't harp on it and whine so much, they might get something changed. I know all their arguments, agree with a lot of what they say, but they just don't seem to understand the world for what it is. Poor Papa thought he could get you away from the bad influences—oh, yes, I do know all about you and that mulatto in Hallsville—"

"If you know so much, call her by her name. *Amaryllis*. She's Amaryllis. *You* can't say *that*, can you? Leave off, Genevra. If Papa were alive, he'd be satisfied. I'm quiet. I doctor—when I have the opportunity to doctor. I run this place—when you give me the opportunity to run this place. I paint sweet pictures extolling the virtues of the local landscape. I'm a good uncle to Mary Tee. I hold up *your* position in the neighborhood—"

"That's just the problem. It's your own position you ought to be studyin'. You sit in this study paintin'. You don't *mix*. You don't take any interest in the mothers' daughters or in anybody except the slaves on this place, and they don't count! Oh, you talk to Mr. Winstead all right, but he's the sheriff. He's a person apart, too. People find you odd. Downright peculiar. I do myself. Papa thought I could help you get over Amaryllis and you could help me get over Jack Tolford's death, but he was wrong. Anyhow, my head's always been better for figures than yours. I guess Papa thought I'd keep this place from losing money, at least. And I have, too. But you don't help me, Sam, not in the deep-down ways that count. I can't fault how you go through the motions. Everybody you tend talks about how nice you are—probably because you won't charge them enough. But it just drives me to distraction that you will not, after two years, *take hold here* and make a life, *live*."

It's small comfort that my oh-so-knowing sister was wrong about one thing. "What I can't understand is how Ho can be the son of Moses. There's never been a better *slave* than Moses. Wonder who the mother was? That must be the problem. Papa bought just the two of them. He didn't like to separate families, so there must have been something wrong with Moses' woman."

She was too much for me, though I couldn't forbear asking her how she thought the slave parents felt when their children were sold away from them to God only knows where.

Moses would have heard of Ho's indiscretion and rebuked him. Amaryllis told me the last time I saw her that he slipped off to train his son against the coming of the GREAT TIME, as they called it among themselves. "I hears 'bout you sassin' Miz Mary Tee. If dat ain't enuff, you gots to mention Mr. Nat Turner, just got to let yo lips flap. Can't stay out here too long widout rousin' suspitshun. An' you be keerful wid dem drums. White folk scairt o' dat drum talk. Dey recollects dat Cato way back dere in Sout Car'lina wit all dem talkin' drums. Kilt thirty White peoples. But we got to use dis time fo' de lessons."

Moses, taught by Amaryllis, as she had been taught by Nat Turner, drilled his son in uprisings. Toussaint L'Ouverture in Haiti with the "Generals" Dessalines and Christophe, inspired by the French Revolution. Gabriel Prosser, Denmark Vesey. Closer to home, because he was a free-born Negro from Wilmington before he moved to Boston, was David Walker.

Amaryllis had extensive quotes from his *Appeal* written out in the diary she gave me that last time we met. I can't get them out of my head. "Can our condition be any worse? . . . The whites have always been an unjust, jealous, unmerciful, avaricious and blood-thirsty set of beings, always seeking after power and authority." But she also cited George Moses Horton's "On Liberty and Slavery" and "our own" Thomas Paine's *The Age of Reason* and John Adams's words of July 4, 1826: "Independence now and Independence forever!" Ole Nat was Ho's favorite: "Gonna be signs in de heavins. Ole Nat be man of signs. Be prophet. Ole Prophet Nat. He pass de word."

Moses had "call and response" born into his blood, was ever the Choragus. "When Colonel Amorillis giv de word, we killem here in Wosaw and Kenan'villes, we killem all in Duplin County, we killem all in Sampson County."

Ho would have responded in the prescribed fashion: "Killem in Mista Duplin, killem in Mista Sampson. Killem all!"

It was as if the very air blew about words of uprising and rebellion. As if we were infected. Even the no-see-um's were the worst that summer anyone had ever known them to be. Omens and foreshadowing as much as any Greek tragedy. And we did not heed them. I remember Abner's words the first time he visited after the infamous tea party. "For a man who prides himself on being the quietest human bein' in these parts, Sam, you have stirred up one fine hornets' nest." It was all there. I should have heard it. But I was so proud. Why, I was proving that slaves had brains, could learn, create . . . The irony was that they were smarter than I gave them credit for being. On the verandah of Freedom Hall, performing for guests Sister Genevra had invited to tea to prove that I "fitted in," I'd expected Moses and his son to perform music. But he also had a "poem," called it such.

Abner was likening it to the Boston and Edenton Tea Parties, when we were interrupted by the loathsome Hake Wright "sent here by my fellow citizens to get to the bottom of this plot and see what this 'darky lover' has to say about it." Alexander Pearsall had arrived at his house before six o'clock that morning to pass on the news from the freedman Ironwood, who ran the forge at Island Creek. He'd gotten wind of a plot brewing among the Negroes when they asked him to make them weapons.

Then Moses himself came running in with a dispatch: a band of two hundred Negroes might be planning to take Kenansville. Abner sent his deputy to call a meeting of all the men, cautioning that this was likely just another rumor, that whatever it was, it was at the planning stages at the moment. Still, we had to be prepared. They were not to do anything to their Negroes, just watch them. Abner refused to act on Hake Wright's charge that I was a "damned abolitionist" and must be locked up.

Abner made me see the dilemma. "I failed to make you realize how revolutionary your—*our*—views are. You could lose your own life over them. You better pause to think in that direction—and about what will happen to Genevra and Mary Tee if you're on the wrong side. They'll be branded right alongside you."

I was in anguish at the thought of having to choose between Amaryllis and her kind on the one hand and Genevra and Mary Tee on the other. I must get them away, but making Genevra "cut and run" would not be easy. I let that problem ride for the moment, called her in, made her aware of the possibilities, and had her prepare Freedom Hall as if for a siege. Neither of us believed any of our Negroes were involved, but we took precautions. Which house servants could be trusted absolutely? We omitted the field hands altogether. She put the women on the provisions, the men on fortifying the house. We'd empty the smokehouse and any other exterior larders so as not to give aid and comfort to the enemy. I collected all the firearms on the plantation and put them in a special place under my lock and key, giving Genevra, who was a better shot than I was, a pistol to keep with her at all times, primed and ready but for cocking.

I went looking for Amaryllis, overheard Moses and her. "Lookaheyar, you comes here and gots all dis started so's you cud be near dat docter man. He nebber wuz gonna hav you in no legal White woman's way, Girl. He shore Lord ain't now. You've brung misery to all us. I be satisfied enuff wid my lot til you done showed up tellin' me how I's a natural-born leader, be needed in Nat Turner's army. You done change all my satisfaction. I got's to do what you set me on to doin' now, no matter what. Even if I ain't got de stomack fer it." She told him she didn't mean to hurt him, had wanted to punish me and the whole White world and didn't care who she used to do it, but he'd "done sent Ole Nat word by Ho 'bout happenins herebouts. After you busted out dancin' in dat crazy way at Miz Genevra's tea party, I knew fer shore t'weren't no use relyin' on you no mo. Ho be too young to be mixin' in dis stuff. I hope he don't get back here till it all blowed over. We's got to have somebody what kin tells our story."

Moses had something to offer her, even in their desperation. "You too hard on yoself, Girl. You could of set yoself up like dem other mulattos. Made yo way wit your body. Disappeared into de White world maybe. You chose de harder way. And dey may still be some time. I'z still willin', still wantin' to marry up wid you. More den willin' to save you if I can. If you decides to throw in yo lot with me, you kin find me. Or git word to me."

He gave me courage. When he left her, I stepped out of the woods, confronted her, made my offer. She was angry and hurting, said she could take care of herself, that she'd had to learn how to after I went away. "I told you I'd find a way if you would. I never heard from you, never heard anything about you. Papa clamped down tight. But I never forgot you, Amaryllis, not for one moment. And I won't ever either, no matter what happens. But this is foolish. You've got to get away from here. If they get you, I'll do what I can, but I won't be able to help much. They don't trust me. *Please* go. I'm sending Genevra and Mary Tee off to Europe immediately. I can persuade my sister to take you along disguised as her body servant. Then, when arrangements can be made, you could go to Liberia. Maybe sometime I could join you . . . anyhow, I have money for you." She slapped it from my hand and told me then. "Poor fool, you don't really know, do you? 'Papa clamped down tight,' did he? You see, my dearest *Brother*, he was *my* papa, too. He told me as soon as you were gone, and then he set me free, gave me some money, on the condition that I never try to see you again. Only, once he was dead, I didn't quite have to keep my bargain any longer." She thrust what proved to be her diary at me and ran off sobbing.

I was too stunned to follow her. They caught her soon after. Hake Wright would have had his way with her if Abner and his deputies hadn't arrived. Moses burst in, unarmed, and was rapidly dispatching her captors until Sheriff Winstead placed a gun to her head. They took them both to the Lodge Hall, secreted them away. Abner came to me then. He was not opposed to killing them if they were proved guilty, but they must be killed *right*. He wanted to know if I had problems with his approach. My pompous words? "I remain a man of the law. If there's proof, I won't try to do more than beg the mercy of the court. But there has to be proof. *Incontrovertible* proof. So far, all we have is *suspicion*."

We'd been on guard two days. The women and children had spent the last two nights in the courthouse cellar under guard, leaving behind the slaves they trusted to look after the houses. Sheriff Winstead had notified the governor. The militia was on alert. The alleged "plot leaders," Moses and Amaryllis, having been taken, the county judge appointed a temporary court of five magistrates. I was among them. Abner meant to make sure that neither I nor any other slaveholder had grounds to sue. "And you have to understand," he said solemnly, "that your neighbors must see you with them—or they'll see you dead." I had just made my peace with it on the grounds that I could best help Moses and Amaryllis from a position of authority when Hake Wright made his baleful entry: "Sheriff, Mr. Coop Hollister just rode up! Says it ain't two hunderd but *two thousand* blacks, an' they're on the Warsaw road headin' towards Kenansville and the courthouse! Says they're massacreeing the Whites indiscriminately! Says he has no doubt they intend rescuin' their leaders, Moses and that high yaller girl, from the jail house!" The die was cast. Horrible, horrible word play. And too true.

Abner had the women and children taken to the top floor of the courthouse. We put them in the center of the room and made a circle around them with chairs. Moses and Amaryllis were moved to the judge's antechamber. If worst came to worst, we would need to trade them. We had already cut a trench around the courthouse, all the available men filling it. Typically, Abner remembered to ask Parson Stanford to stand by and pray for us.

I have been incapacitated since the denouement, though am now well enough. The recovery of my equanimity is far more in doubt. In the retrospect of several months, I still shudder to recall the images that possessed me, and eventually turned to my painting to purge them. I know myself part of what twisted Amaryllis. I loved her deeply and believe the same of her feelings for me. Only the horrors of the institution of slavery could have brought my gentle Amaryllis to declare in her diary, "At Nat Turner's signal as delivered by me, we will commence the horrid work of murder of all the whites without respect to age or sex."

Once Amaryllis brought the word from the insurrectionist Nathaniel Turner in Virginia, Moses was to kill us; and the leader in Sampson County, Mr. James Wright's Pompey, was to kill *his* masters. These murders would be the signal for the uprising here. They had hoped for July 4, for its meaning to us. They would march south to Wilmington, where they would be joined by fifteen hundred more Negroes. Then they would march northwest through Fayetteville and turn north to take Raleigh. Virginia and North Carolina were to be the center of a Negro empire.

I never gave up Amaryllis's diary or told what I knew, but, as a result of the talk she occasioned by her performance at the tea party, she fell under Abner's watchful eye and called attention to the unfolding events. She *and* Moses were brought up on a felony and committed to jail to await Superior Court. Alas, that was not to be. Hake Wright and his ruffians broke in. Although Moses had refused to talk to prevent his own torture, his tongue loosened when his assailants turned to Amaryllis with whipping and more horrible threats. He admitted the murder of Ironwood and gave up names of those who had engaged in the plot. The grand jury found a true bill against six. Three were ultimately convicted and sentenced to die on the eighth of October. Two denied knowing anything of the intended insurrection. One said he had not had a fair trial and that what he said was beat out of him. One was committed for perjury. Two were hanged. One was ultimately pardoned by the Governor. One of our good citizens proposed that Moses and Amaryllis be killed forthwith. Even Abner felt that, if there was a large force coming to release them, we were "justified" in destroying them. His reasoning was cogent: "Either Moses *and* Amaryllis must be killed, or they *and* he *and* any other imagined White sympathizers and all the rest of the Negroes to be found *would* be killed."

The horror. Abner and I having been secured in a cell, Moses and Amaryllis were taken out of jail and shot dead near its back door. I do not know who was executed first but hope that it was Amaryllis and that her horror was foreshortened. But the image conjured by my artist's eye gives the lie to such a hope. That I did see Amaryllis once again I now have to admit, to my everlasting discomfiture. Oh, I have asked God to let this horror pass from me, but it will not be. On Freedom Hall's gateposts were the heads of Amaryllis and Moses. I fetched items from Genevra's linen closet, encased those blind heads, and buried them. The bodies I never recovered. I hope to be able to mark the graves at some time in the future. Genevra, bless her, believes that the story told in my paintings must become a family legacy. Mary Tee will pass it to her children, and it will travel through time.

The horror of horrors. The day following the deaths of Amaryllis and Moses, Abner's outriders returned, having ascertained the facts of the report of the uprising. It was unfounded, mere phantasmagoria! There was no assemblage of Negroes, though the plot was "meditated."

God's irony is great. Recently in Virginia, a man built a *reaper*, a harvesting machine. At the same time, the *Grim Reaper* was at work there when Nathaniel Turner, with his followers, rose up and killed fifty-five Whites before he was caught and hanged. But if you and I can yet see through that Wrath and this Horror such word play on *reaper* and *Grim Reaper*, is there not hope for the minds and the souls who could so cleverly hide "N-a-t" under "g-n-a-t"? But even had I guessed that Moses' poem so played on words, I would not have known what to make of the "N-a-t." I will hear Moses forever. "Dis heyar be poem call 'Ole Nat Be a Worrisome Thing.'"

Ole Nat be a worrisome thing.
Slippin' up on 'em when dey least expect.
Worryin' and worryin' lak a dog wid a bone,
A cat wid a rat, a snake wid a coon.
Seem lak God be usin' dat Ole Nat
To remind us uv our sins, punishin' us now an' den.
Yessuh, Ole Nat be a worrisome thing.
Ole Nat he come from nowheres dey kin tell.
Ole Nat he come quiet till he swarm.
Den dey feels lak dey bein et alive.
Raw Hide an' Bloody Bones hissef
An' all de toments uv Job,
Be after dere flesh.
It be burnin' lak Hellfire,
Dont's believe it to stop till dey daid.
What's to do 'bout Ole Nat?
Ain't much dey kin do.
De mo' dey swats, de mo' dey be's.
(Bees ain't as bad as Ole Nat.)
Ole Nat come when it his time.
Ole Nat come lak a thief in de night.
Ole Nat come lak de sun in de day.
Ole Nat come when it Gawd's time.
Ole Nat begat prodigus Little Nats.
De world, by 'n' by, be tuk ober by Ole Nat!
Yessuh, Ole Nat be a worrisome thing!

The fruits of this dark harvest, which the newspapers are pleased to call "The Duplin Insurrection," are sour. White is more suspicious of Negro than ever before and is increasingly vigilant. Nathaniel Turner, though of Virginia, was a Baptist preacher, and our own state is about to pass legislation to prevent not only slaves but free Negroes from preaching. And the influence of the antislavery forces in North Carolina is greatly reduced. It remains to be seen if this Nathaniel, Amaryllis, Moses, and all the others will amount to more than the bite of a gnat swatted into Kingdom Come. But I can't help remembering "The more they swat, the more there be."

I am more sanguine about the human spirit in general than about my own in particular. Ho suddenly reemerged, his words a message of guileless hope. "I bin mostly in de root cellar from de time I back in dese parts. I specks I shouldn't be outen here, but I donts keer. I's tired o' bein' shut up. I needs Mista Sun. I needs de air thru dese here big ole pecan trees. I ain't plottin' no meanness. I's jist wantin' to play in de sun one mo' time. Ain't even no squirrels been scampin' herebouts since de bad times starts. Blue jays ain't fussin' nuther. When things comin' back? When me an' Miss Mary Tee jumpin' rope again?"

As if on cue, Abner asked Genevra to do him the honor of "jumping rope" with him. "I believe it's called 'jumping the broom' in the quarters. Will you, Miss Genevra, take this old but less-than-solemn man as your husband and partner-at-the-broom?"

At my lowest points, I think of Ho and Mary Tee, children black and white, playing together, and I think of Abner and Genevra happy. My heart feels less heavy.

The Most Beautiful Music

Shirley Nesbitt Sellers

In all of Jenny's life, there had never been such excitement. As soon as the wagon train came in sight, Charlie and Tom came running to the house, shouting the news. Ma rushed past her, wiping her hands on her apron, a broad smile on her face. "Come on, Jenny," she called back over her shoulder. "We should be welcoming them!"

Pa, who never hurried over anything, was already following the boys with long strides, but stopped to wait for Ma to catch up. Jenny suddenly felt shy. She shifted her position on the steps so that she could get a better view of the unusual activities while she peeled potatoes.

Now Pa was with the wagon master, showing him the best place to keep the horses. He still moved as slowly and deliberately as ever, but she saw him remove his broad hat and run his hand over his forehead to the back of his head as he always did when excited or seriously considering something out of the ordinary.

She watched as Charlie stopped to have a word with Pa and then go off on his long legs to give some help and directions. He stopped again when a pretty girl with shiny black hair suddenly jumped down from a wagon directly onto the path in front of him. How wonderful it would be to have hair like that instead of the carroty top on her own head!

Jenny stopped peeling and watched as a sparkling smile brightened the girl's pretty face. The smile held an unusual sweetness, as though to ease the shock Charlie was plainly experiencing as he stood still before her all flustered and red in the face. A lump rose in Jenny's throat at the grown up way Charlie smiled and nodded his rusty head at the lovely interruption.

Luke, the youngest of Jenny's three brothers, broke up the little drama with an impatient tug on Charlie's sleeve. Tom, too, ran by, shouting for Charlie to come on. After a few stammered words that

Jenny couldn't hear, Charlie went on his way, but slowly, and not without several glances back to assure himself that he had not been dreaming.

Now Ma was heading back to the house with six tired-looking women and what looked like a whole schoolroom full of children. Jenny stood politely, but wondered what to say as the chattering children crowded around her, excited and demanding attention. The Stockton family's whole world, for all of Jenny's eleven years, had consisted of the Jennings family who lived two miles north of the schoolhouse, the Williamses five miles west of their own home, and the handful of boys and girls who made their way to the cabin schoolhouse during the winter months when the weather allowed.

She felt the heat rise in her cheeks as Ma introduced her. Somehow she felt important because this was her home, and all these other people were, for the present, homeless. A visit from a wagon train had happened once before, long ago when she was very small. She remembered the bustle and talking, the petting and attention she had received, but that was before the need and yearning to have visitors had become so acute. She wondered how her home would feel to her with so many strangers in and around it. Thinking of the wagons and the only home these people knew right now, she felt suddenly proud of her house. Pa had built it larger than most homes this far west. The last schoolmaster but one had sent some pretty material to Ma when he left for more schooling on the east coast. He had written that it was to thank her for making him so welcome. The curtains sewn from the material made the big family room seem almost elegant.

Jenny could see that Ma was proud of her as she began to play her part of being hostess when she opened the door and held it for the crowd of visitors. There was time before supper for naps for the young children on pallets spread on the floor, and Jenny led the older ones to the garden to pick the vegetables Ma had asked her to fetch for supper.

As they passed one of the wagons, Jenny caught her breath at the lovely music coming from it. The sound sent prickles up the nape of her neck and made her catch her breath. Her surprise must have shown, because a small boy in the group of children around her laughed and said, "That's Sue, showin' off her pianny!" He jumped up on the wagon, stuck his head inside, and called, "Hey, Sue! How about showin' Red here your pianny?"

The music stopped and the pretty black-haired girl looked out, smiling. Behind her Jenny could see a head, russet-colored, Charlie's, she knew. Then Tom's face, too, grinned down at her and all three were laughing and pulling her up to see and hear the wonderful instrument.

Jenny's world was changed in a twinkling. For days, she could hardly be torn from the piano. The James family insisted on letting her keep it in the house, and Sue was a willing teacher. She explained to Jenny how to play notes together to form chords, and taught her many simple songs to sing and to play. She even had books to share that helped Jenny learn about finger positions and the notes of the scale and all manner of things she had never heard of before. Jenny spent so much time with the piano that her usually patient mother became cross with her for not taking care of her assigned chores.

Pa and the boys were in their glory during that time, talking and working with other people. Jenny was vaguely aware of it and felt happy for them. She knew her mother was enjoying the company of other women, too, but she was so immersed in her own floating world of music that the comings and goings of all others were like drifting dreams on the periphery of her own dynamic reality.

Once, it was true, Pa came in looking so white and rubbing his head so intently that she stopped playing long enough to run outside to discover what had happened to bother him. But all she could see was Sue leading off two little boys for lunch and laughing over her shoulder at Charlie. Charlie was just standing there with his arms crossed across his chest, watching her and laughing.

Ma and Pa talked in low, worried whispers that night. Jenny, straining her ears, could barely hear them mention the Jameses and Sue. She knew they were discussing where the wagon train was headed and where it would be going. That brought Jenny around to thinking about the piano. She felt tears on her eyelids at the thought of having to give it up.

On the morning of the day the wagon train was supposed to leave, catastrophe struck. As Jenny threw off an uneasy sleep and tried not to remember what was making her feel so depressed, she lay mesmerized by a sound she had never heard before. Ma was crying! She strained to hear more. Charlie was speaking in low, pleading tones and said something about the wagon train waiting one more day before leaving. Then his words reached her clearly.

"Ma, you must have known that I'd be leaving some day."

Charlie leaving? Jenny jumped from her bed. In her haste she almost tumbled down the loft ladder, screaming, "Charlie! Charlie!"

She flung herself into his open arms, tearfully pleading, "Charlie, don't leave! Please don't leave!"

His arms enclosed her, and, hugging her more tightly than he ever had before through all those big brother years, he sat down on the nearest chair and held her. Somehow Jenny knew that this strong embrace was his answer. He was really leaving!

Through a haze she saw her mother wipe away her tears and start preparing breakfast. Pa left his chair to lend a hand, stopping to pat Ma's shoulder as he passed her. It was with mixed feelings that Jenny saw her mother smile. It relieved her a little, but she couldn't see how any of them could ever smile again if Charlie left.

Tom came in, wiping the early dew from his boots at the doorway. He glanced around at the long faces. Luke followed and stopped short as he also took in the scene.

"What's wrong?" he asked Tom.

Tom, never for long dismayed, shook his head and answered, "Look, Luke. Did you ever before see such a bunch of gloomies?"

Charlie laughed and held Jenny at arm's length, tilting his head and making a funny face at her. Jenny knew he expected a responding laugh, but she could only whisper, "Why are you leaving, Charlie?"

"Because I've found my girl, honey, and I want to travel with her to the ends of the earth!"

Then Jenny remembered yesterday. Pa's white face. Sue laughing over her shoulder. She thought about Sue's anxious willingness to be in the house, near her and Ma while she gave the piano lessons.

The piano! Jenny had thought she couldn't stand to lose the piano. Now she was losing Charlie as well, and she just knew her heart would surely break before this day was through.

But Charlie looked so happy, and then, in a sudden moment, so anxious about his little sister's misery, that she managed to reach up and silently pat his face before making a dive for the loft and the sanctuary of her own pillow.

"Let her go, Charles," she heard Ma say. "She's having a hard time losing the piano and now you, too." Then Jenny heard her say very softly, "She'll learn soon enough that the most beautiful music in the world is a man and a woman finding and loving each other."

"Sarah!" she heard Pa saying a low voice. Then Charlie and Tom and Luke were laughing and teasing their parents as they grabbed their plates. The familiar sounds did nothing to relieve her misery, and no one tried to coax her down to eat.

That night, after all preparations had been made for the next day's journey, a goodbye party was held in the big family room. There was time now for real conversation and a strengthening of old and new family ties before the departure. The travelers were excited and buoyant about the journey ahead. Especially ecstatic were Charlie and Sue. Everyone delighted in their happiness.

The family staying behind pretended to be happy, too. Ma and Pa both chatted and laughed. Once in a while, though, Pa put an arm around Ma and gave her a hug, and her smile would fade a moment as they looked into one another's eyes.

Tom was unusually quiet, Jenny noticed. He stayed close to Charlie, watching the glowing face while his own reflected an uncustomary dejection that was a direct contrast.

It grew late. Little heads slumped forward and back again with stay-awake jerks. Jenny saw Sue go quietly to the piano and stand caressing it gently with her fingertips. Jenny knew it would be the last thing to be loaded onto the wagon tomorrow.

Everyone grew quiet as all eyes turned to Sue who had stood up suddenly and smiled all around at everyone. Jenny felt her breath catch at the lovely picture she made. It seemed to Jenny that Sue looked a little wistful and she wondered if perhaps plans had been changed and Charlie was not leaving after all. But then Sue came across the room and stooped gracefully in front of the chair where Ma was sitting. She took her future mother-in-law's hand and held it against her own flushed cheek. Ma moved her hand farther up to stroke the dark hair.

"Take care of him, Sue," she entreated.

Sue stood then and looked at Jenny. Turning back to Ma, she said brightly, "I'm going to leave the piano, Mrs. Stockton. I'm going to leave it with Jenny. And some day, not too far off, Charlie and I will come back to get it. When you hear Jenny playing, you can remember this promise."

Jenny tried to move toward Sue, but her feelings held her motionless. All the pent up emotions of the day were crowding in upon her. Her lips trembled and through her tears she saw Sue walk over and stand before Pa. With a little nervous giggle, she looked up into his serious, kindly face.

"A piano isn't much of a trade for a wonderful son, is it, Mr. Stockton?"

Pa ran his hand over his head and smiled down into her anxious eyes. "Well, it can't pull a plow around, for sure. But it can pull at a man's heartstrings and keep him going."

Then Sue walked over to Jenny who was still bleary-eyed and speechless. Smiling, she gave Jenny a hug. "Practice hard," she said, "and when we come to get it you'll be such a success we'll have to take you back with us."

Jenny swallowed. Searching Sue's face, she whispered, "Are you sure?"

"That I'm leaving it for you? Oh, yes. There won't be much time for me to play it, and you really have a talent I'd like to see blossom."

Over Sue's shoulder, Jenny saw Charlie approaching with his familiar grin.

"Hey, little one, how about a smile after you've been given such a real nice gift?"

Jenny found herself clinging to Charlie, crying and laughing all at once. How could Sue part with her precious piano? Her love for Charlie must include his family, too.

She felt herself taken by the hand as Sue led her over to the piano with Charlie in tow. When she looked up and saw the two faces smiling first at her and then at each other, she decided she really could hear the most beautiful music that Ma had been talking about that morning.

About the Authors

The Red Dress

Matt Cutugno was born in Perth Amboy, New Jersey, and educated at Pennsylvania State and Florida State Universities. His plays have been produced in New York and Los Angeles; his prose has been published in the Manhattan literary journal *Words*, in Brooklyn's *Si Senor*, in the Canadian magazines, *Freefall* and *Qwerty*, and in the *Dan River Anthology*. He is a regular contributor to the e-zine *Hilltop Observer* (http://www.hilltopobserver.com). He has contributed to previous volumes of *In Good Company*, published by Live Wire Press. Matt and his wife Lily live in Manhattan. He can be reached at Cutugno@msn.com

Conrad's Passage

Don Amburgey is a teacher, drama producer, and a regional librarian in Kentucky. Numbered among his pastimes are: the loves of music and storytelling, and playing banjo, guitar, and mandolin. However, reading remains his dominant pleasure. His writings include: poetry, stories, and a fictionalized biography called *Constantine Samuel Rafinesque, Solo Naturalist*. With wife Joyce, also a librarian, he lives in Jenkins, Kentucky.

Second Act

Jason Lester Atkins was born in Hampton, Virginia, and attended Huntington School of Engineering and the University of Oklahoma. He was a gunner on a torpedo bomber in WW II. His first published story appeared in *Holiday* magazine in 1950. His published poetry has appeared in *The Poet's Domain, Borders, Writer's Voice, Beacon*, and *West Virginia Review*. He is now retired and is facilitator of the Virginia Beach Writer's Group.

The Gardener

Terry Cox-Joseph freelances from her home in Newport News, Virginia. She is a member of the Poetry Society of Virginia and has been published in *Chiron Review, The Poet's Domain, The Blotter,* and *Prairie Poetry,* among others. She won the 2005 Judah, Sarah, Grace, and Tom Memorial Contest from the Poetry Society of Virginia, and an honorable mention in the 2006 *Writer's Digest* nonfiction category. She is a former newspaper reporter and editor and has had one book of nonfiction published, *Adjustments* (Hampton Roads, 1993). From 1994–2004 she was the coordinator for the annual Christopher Newport University Writers' Conference and Contest. She displays and sells her watercolors, acrylics, and oils at Blue Skies Gallery in Hampton, Virginia, a membership fine-art gallery.

The Day a Crow Snatched My Baby Sister

Pete Freas is a Chesapeake poet and publisher. He maintains a poetry events website (www.chcsbaypoets.org) and publishes a weekly online newsletter, A Line in Time, issued every Sunday. He also edits *Skipping Stones,* an annual anthology of Hampton Roads poets, artists, and photographers. His chapbooks include *Haiku* (a collection of 52 of his short poems), *Boots* (poems reflecting his Vietnam experience as a helo gunship pilot), and *60-60 Goin' Strong* and *Gettin' On to 60 and Beyond.* His poetry has appeared in *The Open Page, The Poet's Domain,* and *Poetica.*

Pete's initiatives and efforts in support of poetry and the arts earned him the coveted Alli Award from the Cultural Alliance of Hampton Roads in 2007. He is often found as MC at open-mic and open-reading events across Hampton Roads, including regular monthly readings at The Book Owl in Portsmouth, Prince Books in Norfolk, and the Peninsula Fine Arts Center in Newport News. He has been featured at Iris Art Shop, the Poetry Society of Virginia Saturday Series, the Phoebus Art Factory; he is a member of CNU Writers' Council, Hampton Roads Writers, and Poetry Society of Virginia where he serves as VP of the Southeastern Region.

Pete and his wife live in Chesapeake. Their daughter is a defense contractor in Washington, D.C., and their son, a digital imaging engineer for Canon, lives in Portsmouth.

About the Authors

The Door of Randolph Manor

Stephanie Friar: the youngest of nine children, was born to John and Dathine Cook, of Ada, Oklahoma. She graduated from Ada High School and attended Southeastern Oklahoma State University for a time, majoring in music. She has a bachelors degree in Biblical Studies from Southwestern Christian University in Bethany, Oklahoma.

She currently works as a Military Personnel Specialist, and has proudly served the fine men and women of the United States Navy for more than eight years. She is also the Minister of Music at Southside Vineyard Community Church.

A lover of U.S. history, she and her family spend their spare time as reenactors of the Revolutionary War and the War of 1812 with the Seventh Virginia Regiment, Virginia State Navy; and the War of 1812's Second Virginia Regiment.

She is an avid reader and began writing her own stories a little over three years ago. She is currently working on a book of short stories and a novel. She lives in historic Smithfield, Virginia, with her husband Rob and their three children Sean, Jeremiah, and Madeline.

Sitting on Plastic

Doris Gwaltney is the author of *Homefront, Shakespeare's Sister, Duncan Browdie, Gent, A Mirror in Time.* She has had poetry and short fiction included in *The Greensboro Review, In Good Company, The William and Mary Review, The Poet's Domain, Virginia Adversaria, Cube,* the *Beacon,* and others. She teaches a writing class for the LifeLong Learning Society at Christopher Newport University.

The Pony That Looked West
Watch Birds

Elaine J. Habermehl is a writer of short fantasy stories. She likes to take an ordinary situation and inject a little mystery or magic into it. She is fond of a surprise ending, one that will cause a lump in your throat, a laugh, or just an "I didn't see that coming" reaction. Her creativity comes from the natural world, music, and the antics of her fellow humans.

She has been published in literary magazines in the United States and Canada and reads her work in a monthly literary salon and to small groups at the local library. She belongs to the National League of American Pen Women. Elaine is a native Washingtonian and makes her home in Maryland.

Rainy Night in Wilhering

Keppel Hagerman was born in Richmond, Virginia. She is a graduate of Duke University, and also attended writers' workshops in Virginia Commonwealth University; Richmond, Virginia, Old Dominion University, Norfolk, Virginia, and the University of Virginia, Charlottesville, Virginia.

During her husband's thirty-year naval career, she and their three children lived in Germany, Paris, Washington, D.C., Norfolk, Virginia, and Seoul, Korea, where she taught English to Korean children in orphanages.

The Husky Young Man and the Nun

Robert L. Kelly's story comes from his first day visiting New Orleans. While resting on a bench in Jackson Square, a nun and a husky young man joined him, giving him the perfect opening of a story. Bob began writing twelve years ago with Doris Gwaltney and Heidi Hartwiger in the LifeLong Learning Society's program at Christopher Newport University. He continues classes with Heidi. Bob also continues to serve on the board of Christopher Newport University's Writers Conference and Writing Contest, enjoying the excitement of that great annual event.

Bob and his wife Peggy, live near the James River in Newport News. Two of their sons and two grandchildren live in Newport News. Their other two sons and grandchildren live in Bristow and Minneapolis.

The Caregiver

M. L. Kline is a freelance writer who resides in the woodlands of Delaware. Her poetry has appeared in volumes 23 and 24 of *The Poet's Domain*. Other works were included in *Bride's Mountain*, the *Catholic Digest, Family, Ladycom, Pulpsmith*, the *Air Force Times, Selma Times Journal*, and the *Dover Post*.

The Monkey Man
The Left Ascension

D. S. Lliteras is the author of ten books, which have received national and international acclaim. In the last twenty years, his poetry and short stories have appeared in numerous periodicals and anthologies. His most recent novel, *The Master of Secrets*, was published in March 2007

About the Authors

Summer 1956

Jim Meehan is a lifelong resident of the Tidewater, Virginia, area and presently resides in a circa 1920 home by the Lafayette River in Norfolk. He graduated from Maury High School and began an apprentice program at the Norfolk Naval Air Station, fulfilling his desire to work on airplanes.

He started a program to train as an engineer after four years of apprentice school and nine years working on navy aircraft on the aircraft line and emergency repair teams. He qualified as an industrial engineering technician and an industrial engineer with the Naval Facilities Engineering Command. He contributed to projects for the Defense Department in the U.S. and overseas and was fortunate to be able to travel to many parts of the world.

He has written non-fiction articles on the subject of aviation history, which were published in magazines and journals. He has been an avid reader since childhood and has been writing fictional short stories and poetry since retiring from engineering. To learn more about fiction writing, he took courses in English composition and creative writing at Old Dominion University and Tidewater Community College campuses in Virginia Beach, Norfolk, and Chesapeake.

His poetry was published in several issues of *Skipping Stones,* the poetry journal of the Chesapeake Bay Poets and *44th Street*, published by an Old Dominion University poets group. *Vendetta*, his novel set in Sicily during early World War II, is finished and looking for a publisher.

From a Distance, through the Foliage
No Danger to Self or Others

Anne Meek is a retired educator originally from Tennessee, who moved to Alexandria, Virginia, in 1987 to serve as managing editor *of Educational Leadership* at the Association for Supervision and Curriculum Development. Prior to that, she had edited *Tennessee Educational Leadership* while serving as principal and supervisor in Knoxville. As a principal, she invited Rodney Jones (now at Southern Illinois University) to serve as a poet in the school; as a supervisor, she provided the same program to local schools. She was a member of the Knoxville Writers Workshop for several years.

Anne has recently been appointed to the board of the Cultural Alliance of Greater Hampton Roads, housed in Norfolk, Virginia. She also serves as an associate editor for *Skipping Stones,* the regional poetry and art anthology edited and published by Pete Freas at Mindworm Press in Chesapeake, Virginia. She is a member of The Poetry Society of Virginia and a volunteer for poetry-in-the-schools projects.

Anne is descended from writers on both sides of her family. Her maternal grandfather, Thomas Jefferson Campbell, was the author of *The Upper Tennessee* (reissued as *Steamboats on the Tennessee*) and *Records of Rhea.* A paternal aunt, Effie Meek Maiden, was the author of *Home in the Wilderness,* a family history written like a novel, covering the years 1848–1878. Anne's son writes short stories about camping in the Smoky Mountains; and her daughter, the author of *Sweet Invisible Body,* teaches creative writing at the University of Central Florida. Anne's first novel is underway, as is a biography of her father, Paul Meek, former chancellor of the University of Tennessee at Martin.

Josie Higgins

In her many incarnations, Lu Motley has been a soloist with several churches in Richmond, and has performed with the Virginia Museum Theater as Buttercup in *HMS Pinafore* and as Mrs. Beauchamp in *Three Penny Opera,* as well as the farmer's wife in *Mother Courage.* Her play, *Mom and Min,* was performed in 1987 at Theater IV in Richmond.

Formerly, Lu taught English and speech, three years at Rappahannock Community College; before that she taught for twelve years at J. Sargeant Reynolds Community College in Richmond. Lu has three grandchildren, Jessica, Cody, and Jozepha.

When Fate Comes Calling

Sandra Ratcliff is a thirty-four-year-old single mother of two boys, Bubba, thirteen, and Stephen, seven. They live in Portsmouth, Virginia. Sandra's large extended family, who live nearby, have all been extremely supportive of her writing. Each member has also helped to inspire a lot of Sandra's writings, as well as her two boys who have been made into characters many times in her stories and books. She gives them thanks and all of her love for all their inspiration and support, as well as their patience and understanding

Seeing her husband and best friend die at the young age of twenty-nine taught her to never take one day for granted and to live every day to its fullest; never afraid to pursue her passions and dreams.

Sandra and her boys are very active in the local community theater. To sum up, Sandra gives thanks to the one person whose presence in her life gives her the passion, talent, drive, determination, strength, and patience to pursue her writing. That person is God, who has blessed her with many wonderful people to love and support her and with more blessings than she can even list.

"With God, all things are possible." Matthew 19:26

Needin' Mista Sun

Former college president Dr. Lynn Veach Sadler has published widely in academics and creative writing. Editor, poet, fiction/creative nonfiction writer, and playwright, she has published several chapbooks and won the *Pittsburgh Quarterly*'s Hay Prize, the Poetry Society of America's Hemley Award, and *Asphodel*'s Poetry Contest and tied for first place in *Kalliope*'s Elkind Contest. One story appears in Del Sol's *Best of 2004 Butler Prize Anthology*; another won the 2006 Abroad Writers Contest/Fellowship (France). A novel will soon join her novella and short-story collection, and she was named 2007 Writer of the Year by California's elizaPress. She won the 2009 overall award (poetry and fiction) of the San Diego City College National Writer's Contest and *City Works Journal*. A play on Frost was a *Pinter Review* Prize for Drama, Silver Medalist, and she won the 2008 Pearson Award at Wayne State for a play on the Iraq war.

The Most Beautiful Music

Shirley Nesbit Sellers is a retired teacher of Norfolk schools, resides in Norfolk, and is active in storytelling and in story and poetry workshops. She has won numerous awards in the Poetry Society of Virginia and the Irene Leach Memorial contests; was second place winner in the National Federation of State Poetry Societies Poetry Manuscript contest (1977) and has published a chapbook, *Where the Gulls Nest: Norfolk Poems* (Ink Drop Press).